DOWN LOW
SISTER
ON TOP

I0561400

Celebrating The African
American Bisexual Woman

Jenise Justice Brown

Inc.

Editorial services provided by Patricia R. Corbett for JUSTaSISTA

Copyright and Monica Chambers © 2014, 2015, 2023 Jenise Inc.

ISBN: 978-0-9904187-5-7(reprint)

Cover Art by Darryl Jones Photography and Jenise Inc. Cover Art © 2023

I dedicate this book to my family and friends who watched me lament over relaunching and continued to encourage me. Thanks for respecting my flow and being the catalyst for my unending push toward a better world

CONTENTS

Preface

Before writing this book, I traveled to the United States looking for women who, like me, have been living in the intersection of being black, bisexual, female, and silenced by society. I searched the internet first but only found hook-up sites. I quickly realized I would have to seek them out another way.

I began asking black women in the LGBTQ+ if they identified as bisexual. The next step was getting those who said yes, to trust me enough to answer some basic questions. Once trust was established I was able to share my vision for a more inclusive society. I shared some of my journey with them. They, in turn, shared their stories with me. In telling my story I felt a huge weight lift off my shoulder and the walls to keep people out started crumbling. It was difficult to be so vulnerable. My goal became very clear, I wanted the women to gain their freedom. I believe storytelling is a path to get there.

I shared with all the women my story of having a crush on a male and a female at the same time. They could relate to keeping things on the low when you're afraid of how the world may treat you if they knew your truth. After that story, women were willing to share their experiences without prompting. However, to my dismay, many of them were not interested in being the poster child for bisexuals.

The fear of blowing up your life; in church, on the job, and within your family was too great. I shared with them the benefits I saw in them leading the way for tolerance and acceptance but I knew the risk for some, outweighed the reward. Particularly in a world, in a system, that thrives on using what makes us different as a weapon to control an agenda toward separatism hatred

When I began compiling my notes, I focused on creating training that could help women take back their voices or uncover a voice they didn't know they had. I called it Create Your Big Picture. My experience in the entertainment and film industries helped me understand the various roles one could play in creating a story for a screen or stage correlated to the roles we play in creating the life we wanted to live. My goal was to raise the ceiling on possibilities. But I was sidetracked by a bigger picture for the training. The stories by themselves were the sparks for change in the women that shared them but also for me. Every telling of my own story released fear's grip.

I spent months preparing the training and had begun putting the pieces into place to launch it when I shared some of the stories with one of my many mentors, Micheal Ajakwe, founder of LAWEBFEST, He was intrigued by the subject and suggested I put a pin in the idea for the workshops/training and focus on writing a book first to tell the stories. I trusted Mike's judgment so I did.

Christmas Eve 2013, the manuscript was completed. Mike and I celebrated this first milestone and made plans to get together after publishing, I rushed to publish making all the rookie mistakes. I was happy with the reception but it felt a little incomplete so I pulled it from the shelves. At the time a critic said there was too much focus on sex in it. I contemplated relaunching it without the sex. Then it occurred to me, sex is one of the most controlling tools dominant culture has used to limit a woman's freedom of expression. But more importantly, sexual intimacy when shared from a place of pure vulnerability allows all human beings to experience depths no other human connections can offer. The deeper aspect of our connections is where change happens. Mike transitioned before we got a chance to complete that script but I will get it done.

Introduction

Eve-Olusion of Justice Stone

Down Low Sister #1

I 've been honored to interview many prominent people. In my twenty years of experience, a person's popularity weighs very little when I sit down with them. I'm interested in the person, not the personality. Many people have a difficult time distinguishing between the two. It wasn't until I met Oscar Smith, did I fully grasp how seductive being popular can be if you forget the difference.

My first time with my ex, I woke up fully clothed and immersed with pieces of me inserted into her dream. With Oscar, I woke up completely naked with a blueprint for my own.

Oscar is a philanthropist and the most highly respected producer in television and film. He also has an exclusive mentoring program. I met him at a fundraising gala for child cancer research. We were amongst several speakers and Oscar was the keynote. While waiting in the green room, Oscar began telling stories of his travels and the amazing people he met along the way. Suddenly a staff member came running through the door apologizing profusely. There was a mistake in the program and I was listed as the keynote speaker instead of Oscar. After the staff member caught her breath, Oscar quietly said, "My friend Maya says, people will remember how you made them feel, not if you were the first or last speaker. And some will not remember you at all."

We delivered the keynote speech to a standing ovation. It was magical being on stage with one of the most admired people in the world, My phone started ringing off the hook for future engagements. Everything I have done since that time I attribute to that night.

A few months later I was at a crossroads. My relationship with someone I thought was "the one" was over. The demand for my talent and expertise was growing but my motivation was stuck on heartbreak. When I thought it was time for me to just pull up my bootstraps and fake it, I received a call from Oscar's assistant offering me an opportunity to be one of four people to receive 1 on 1 mentoring with Oscar. I said yes.

Fast forward. Motown sounds are playing in the background. I"m lying face down, ass up, fully clothed on Oscar"s couch. He's straddling me as he rubs the kinks out of my shoulders. I'm talking nonstop about my ex-girlfriend and the pain of loving someone so much it hurts.

"We were perfect and then we weren't." I said.

"Sometimes people have to go so we can grow." He said

I started talking nonstop. Oscar gingerly placed his hand over my mouth.

"You have major work to do, and she can't go with you." Removing his hand, he stood up, "Take off your clothes."

I thought I heard the screeching sound you hear before you drive into a brick wall. Oscar sensed my apprehension.

"I want you to take off your clothes so I can give you a full massage. And, you can keep talking things out."

There was just enough space between him and me

to run if necessary. However, instead of running, I started unbuttoning my jeans. I'm typically shy about my body which is now well over twenty-five. Yet, a little voice said no worries. My voice was a little shaky when I responded with a faint "Okay."I was putty in this man's hands—a total contrast to my staunch position on not letting anyone control me.

"You have a beautiful body," Oscar said, reading my thoughts. The microwave dinged. "I'll be right back, " he said. " Keep talking."

My thoughts were racing. My dad taught me to anticipate the dangers of new situations. I didn't feel unsafe vibes coming from Oscar, but many maniacs appear safe. Physically, he towered over me, but I'm a certified Tai Chi practitioner. I could take him down. Oh my God! Am I being punked? Will my naked body be all over the internet? I did a quick scan of the room for hidden cameras.

Oscar entered the room as I was settling my chi. When I saw him, my jaw hit the floor. There he stood, butt-ass naked, with a towel in one hand and a bowl in the other.

Seeing the obvious shock on my face, Oscar tried to make light of the moment.

"No worries, I'm the only one who will see this." He teased.

"What? I knew it. Where is the camera?"

"Relax, J. I'm just kidding." Said Oscar placing the bowl on the table.

"I don't know if I can believe you now?"

"Oh, come now, girl," he said.

His tone was soothing and I felt very comfortable. Maybe it was how he looked at me. His Ethiopian heritage and large oval eyes had me hypnotized. Perhaps I was intoxicated from the aroma of sandalwood and vanilla emitted from the bowl he once carried. Whatever it may have been, I decided to go with it.

"Go on. Lay down." Oscar directed me to the towel he had placed on the couch. I tried to lower myself but forgot my pants were around my ankles. I tripped and fell into Oscar. He caught me just as my hand brushed across his penis. Oscar laughed without flinching. "Are you okay?"

"I'm good," I said, trying to cover my embarrassment. "Sorry, I slipped."

"You are fine." He leaned in. "Use my shoulder for balance." His skin was hot and smooth as silk. He stood there patiently waiting while I finished removing my pants. When I was done a lowered myself to the couch carefully avoiding touching the gorgeous piece of art that hung before me. I tried to ignore it. The only thing missing was a sign that read,

'Do Not Touch.'

I swear it was priceless.

"Come lay here, Kojo. I got you." Oscar said.

"Kojo?"

"It means beautiful."

"I'm sorry. I'm a little nervous."

"Don't worry; nothing will happen unless you want it. Close your eyes, and start again."

I had not had sex since my breakup almost a year prior. I was turned way up by the possibility of what may come next with this fine-ass brother, but no, we had just met, and I needed to be on guard just in case he was psycho.

"You are overthinking, Kojo. Take a deep breath and speak from your heart. It has a lot to say to you."

The warm oil helped me to relax, and I began to exhale in his hands. I started crying.

"I'm still in love with her, and I don't want that ever to change," I said.

"It will not change, but it can become something more than you can imagine."

That day is still number one on my list of the most erotic nonsexual experiences ever.

Oscar massaged my heart like I envisioned Source Energy doing when I meditate. Every muscle of his body fused with mine as he kneaded me. His hands took me deeper into my past, uncovering layers of pain. Oscar helped me release my resistance to receive what was waiting for me on the other side of the pain. I found joy again and allowed it to shine.

Taking a couple more deep breaths at his prompting, I exhaled into the moment and drifted into my loftiest dreams and desires. When I opened my eyes, Oscar was at his workstation. I joined him at a space he had created just for me. The lighting was perfect. Pinot Noir was chilling in the fridge. Chai was brewing on the stove, and Marvin Gaye sang Here My Dear. Something had shifted in me. I felt the backdrop for what would be the beginning of the rest of my life without HER.

On the flight home, I had déjà vu that and burst into laughter so loud it startled the guy next to me. It struck me how I am such a creature of habit. You see, before working with Oscar I had another mentor on the other side of the world. I met them both through mutual friends at a crucial turning point in my career. And I slept with them on the first night but didn't have sex. The parallels ended there. My first time with her, I woke up fully clothed and immersed with pieces of me inserted into her dream and her life. With Oscar, I woke up completely naked with a blueprint for my own life.

One of the aspects of that life included opening a club catered to women who love men and women. I had been living in the footlocker in the back of the closet. My exes career didn't allow us to be open or out as a lesbian couple and she wasn't comfortable with me being bisexual.

My trip back felt more like a step forward into my true self. Exiting the plane, I locked eyes with a beautiful woman name Avery. We shared small talk and exchanged numbers. She became the first founding member of Club Beijui. India, Samantha, Zoe, Fayemi, Enid, Khaleesi, Lisa, Imani, Keysa, and I are the first members of Club BeiJui.

As a member, we understand that we are at the intersection of loving across boundaries. We sit on the leading edge of true freedom. We know our sexual orientation is connected to our power to affect change toward a more tolerant existence. To maintain our alignment and balance in society, we will develop mastery in one or more of four art forms; **the art of lying, the art of social networking, the art of power of influence, and the art of selfishness.** Each has its own set of challenges that requires her to make difficult decisions. The goal is to lean into authenticity.

The Art of
LYING

TO BE. TO REMAIN UNDISCLOSED OR
UNDISTURBED, BURIED IN A
PARTICULAR PLACE. TO EXIST
To unify around lies of entitlement and
inspire authenticity.

Humankind tells lies all day, every day. There's the flat-out lie that is told when everyone knows you're lying, even you, but you can't stop yourself from telling it. Then there"s the bald-faced lie that flows like water from your lips. It's told with conviction making it easy to believe. And then there's my personal favorite, the three-step lie. The first step is you get caught lying in an email, text message, you were being followed, or a phone call. Step two, you deflect by focusing on how you got caught. Step three the liar becomes the victim and says things like, "If you hadn't been snooping you wouldn't have found anything."

Let's face it, humanoids lie on their taxes, job applications, our children, and our parents. Teachers and preachers do it too. If you say you have never lied, you are lying right now. No worries. Most liars find it hard to admit, and then they develop temporary memory loss when someone lies to them.

There's a shared belief amongst liars that some lies are not as bad as others. They call them little white lies. For some 'unknown reason,' they think putting white in front of it makes it less of a lie. Some liars believe it's okay to tell one if it is to protect someone when in fact it is the truth that shall make you free and it takes but whose truth. Liars seek legitimate outcomes so therein lies the truth. At the core of every lie is someone's true desired outcome that can enable them to conceal themselves, hiding and withdrawing from people who intrude on their comfort zone.

Inside My Head

AVERY.

Being bisexual increases your options to find love. It doubles or quadruples but so are your chances of not finding anyone. For someone like me, it's a hard-knock life because I'm searching for someone to complete me. I haven't found one person that can do that. Besides, being with a woman is different from being with a man. There are different expectations but they both agree on one thing they both desire, and that's me as the aggressor, Damn, that's too much work.

When I married John, I had no intention of ever seeking anyone else, male or female. Once I committed to him, that was it for us both. He knew I was bisexual, and I knew he was a womanizer.

After our second child was born, John's infidelities were a constant problem, literally front-page news because of our status and affiliations. All publicity is good publicity until it threatens to destroy my family. Keeping the family together, appearances, and keeping our careers intact made it possible for me to put out the fires he constantly started without a second thought. When we decided to go into entertainment, we agreed to work out our differences privately. I played by the rules, but John was on another program. Several years after we were wed, I discovered he had contacted his ex the week before. That wasn't nearly as devastating as his affair with his assistant.

According to the book of John, which sounds like an episode of Jerry Springer, the affair was supposed to be a one-time thing. He said he was drunk and she seduced him. However, the seduction on one night spanned a whole year resulting in her becoming pregnant. Of course, he said she lied to him about being on the pill. He claimed she only said it because he was ending it.

Our situation was what shows like Maury Povich and Jerry Springer thrive on. The whole world saw our dirty laundry blowing all over Washington DC. I was livid. Not only did he cheat, but he didn't use protection. He jeopardized my life and my standing in the community. I stayed with him because that is what you do, but I was tired.

John groveled for my forgiveness for weeks. I could only offer him a peace agreement. Number one, I would no longer bury my desires for women and owed him no explanation if I found one to my liking. Number two, if he were ever caught with his pants down again, he would immediately vacate our home and I would get everything. He did not raise an eyebrow until number three. I would get full custody of the children. He tried to argue that he had rights when it came to them, and I couldn't care less. I threatened to do some terrible things to sabotage his career, and he knew I could, so he reluctantly agreed to my terms.

So here I am with this new freedom to explore, yet caught in my feelings about my failed marriage. Our wonderful life flipped inside out with a new baby on the way. The children seemed to manage okay. I had to find an outlet. Ladies-only clubs catering to high-profile women are outside the phone book. After several weeks of research, I found a club called Da Spot. That's where I met Pat. The typical get-to-know-you conversation ensued. She travels to New York once a month several on business. I told her, "My life is full, and I'm just looking for some fun."

"So am I," she said.

"I'm married, but it is over. I still need time to sort some things out."

"I fully understand," she said.

Pat was saying everything right to calm down my nervousness surrounding this new experience. I relaxed, but we could only rendezvous in DC, never New York. John's infidelity taught me many valuable lessons, and most importantly, never shit where you eat. "Not a problem," she said. "This is an election year anyway, and the politicians are what interest the paparazzi."

"That's true, and DC is far enough away from

prying eyes and my family and close enough for me to get home quickly if I need to."

We hooked up the next month, and things appeared to be going well. Spontaneity and flexibility are part of my business and hers, and last-minute business trips provided the backdrop for impromptu getaways without suspicion.

Three months into our relationship, things seemed to be going so well. The home life was pleasant because Pat was helping me keep the edge off while we were going through the paternity suit. I contemplated divorce, but the timing wasn't right. My kids were having a tough time with all the attention. With all his faults, John is still my children's father. I loved him for that, and I wasn't going to abandon him at this low point in his life. Pat knew all of this, so I was surprised when she started asking me questions in the middle of her giving me oral sex.

"When are you going to leave him?" Screaming (inside my head), Yet, I said, "Never."

To her, I asked, "Where is this coming from?"

"I'm in love with you." She said, "I think about you

all the time."

There was more screaming inside my head. "What the freak? You knew the deal from the beginning, strictly sexual relationships. Damn! Damn! Damn!"

To her, in the calmest tone I could muster, I said, "I understand, baby. Can we talk about this later?"

Pat looked like she was about to go postal. I knew I needed to respond quickly or suffer whatever she could potentially do.

"Baby, I'm going to leave," I said.

"I can't do it until the kids are out of the house. I know you deserve more than I'm giving you. I understand if you can't wait. I care about you too much to hold you back."

Inside my head, I was screaming, "Oh my God, this woman is crazy. Avery, get dressed and go home now." With passive resistance, she allowed me to roll her onto her stomach. I reached for the raspberry peaches strategically placed next to the bed and straddled her. The stiffness of her body gave way to the idea of what I was planning to do with the peaches. I put a slice halfway in my mouth. I leaned into her pressing all of my desire into her and inviting her to take the other half.

"We are not finished," she said, opening her mouth. Our lips touched as the juice sealed the kiss.

"I hear you, baby" I whispered looking deep into her eyes. "We can work it out later, but right now, let me love you." I grabbed the peaches and began pouring the juice on her nipples down to her navel. Her hips rhythmically raised and lowered with each drop. Her moans deepened, signaling the release of all thoughts of John and divorce, even if only for the moment. She turned onto her back. I traced the juice into the arch of her back. She twitched with each drop, Some of the juice tried to at each drop even to escape along the side of her body. I quickly licked it off of her before it could touch the bed. Pat arched her back raising her hips. Without warning, I lifted her ass and inserted my tongue into her welcoming vagina.

"Damn, you have never done that before."

"Today is your lucky day," I said.

"Call me lucky charms," she moaned before releasing all her inhibitions in a puddle on the bed. We had progressive orgasmic crescendos all night for both of us. However, in my head, I was scanning ways of ending or affair. She was moving way too fast, which could be a potential problem. My husband and I have an arrangement, and we are committed to our family and all the benefits of being who we are in society. My relationship with someone else will never interfere. I knew this, but I wanted to be free of everything. The time spent with Pat helped me awaken to a little of that freedom.

When I returned home, John was waiting with flowers and another neglige. All part of his attempt to save our marriage. He has no clue that gifts like that are not for women. Unfortunately for him, no gift will suffice. Our marriage has lasted beyond its expiration, and I'm filing for divorce once the kids go to college. I love John, but I don't like or respect him anymore. I never imagined this would be us.

In the meantime, I need to help Pat end our entanglement. I could tell her it's over, but I've never been good at ending anything. And I'm not sure how she would respond. It's been a few months, and she's on some stalker shit now and making demands of my time that I refuse to honor even if I could. She announced she was joining Club Beijui. But she had only been there once when she went with me to a white party. Membership is by invitation only, and I know Justice didn't invite her to join. And she is not bisexual.

In my experience, three months with someone isn't long enough to uproot your It may work for others, but my track record shows otherwise. Women say ninety days with someone means they have passed all the basic tests for being long-term relationship material. Well, not if the time spent is a sexfest. Pat and I do nothing else. I must find a way to do something quickly, or the next scandal will be mine. John doesn't know, but timing is crucial, and she is borderline psychotic. I need to make her end it. I've tried the conveniently unavailable approach and purposefully canceled meet-ups at the last moment. Getting inside her head has been easy. However, getting out may not be.

Suck It Up

INDIA.

After years of cheating and running game, I thought I knew how to handle relationships. I was not prepared for this woman. With her, I was in uncharted territory. Everything I wanted, she easily dismissed. Even when it came Instead of talking thru what I felt was missing, she insisted we needed therapy. All I needed was for her to hear me. Her insistence on therapy felt like she was saying something was wrong with me. I agreed to go because I wanted to fix myself for her, Maybe I was overly needy.

On our very first visit, my red flags went next level. First of all, Dr. Goodman was one of her colleagues and they played golf together. Everybody knows deals are made at bars and on the golf course. How could he be unbiased and he's a cisgender heterosexual white male? What in the hell could he know about the intimacy issues of a black female same-sex relationship? We were already there, so I decided to give him the benefit of the doubt.

Dr. Goodman spent the first 20 minutes getting to know us as a couple. He asked questions like how long we had been together, our family dynamics, and how we met. I let her tell that story even though it is one of my favorites. When she was finished he asked her to step out so he could talk to me alone.

"Why are you here?" He asked. My defenses kicked in. And I was a bit annoyed that he would ask that again."After all, you just heard, you can't figure that out?"I blurted.

Dr. Goodman sat back in his chair. I stared at him, I wanted an answer. He stared back and asked me again." Why are you here?" My frustration peaked. I wanted to run out of there. But I sat there staring at him and the tears began to form in my eyes. I took several deep breaths trying to control the quiver in my stomach.

"I want more intimacy," I said.

Dr. Goodman handed me the box of tissues. His eyes never left mine. He said," I know. And, you are not wrong for wanting it."

Months of feeling ashamed for daring to want more came pouring out of me at that moment. I started looking forward to meeting with Dr. Goodman. He recommended some books for us. I read them and practiced the principles they offered. She didn't read anything and still held intimacy hostage. I decided to pretend everything was fantastic. I was the only one I could not fool. Here is our story.

The love of my life, my queen, doesn't see me. I placed her on a pedestal from day one, and I didn't know that doing so was setting her up for failure. Her father tried to warn me as he observed how much I catered to her on holiday visits. My Queen's ego was alive and running her life, and I co-signed every word.

Her father would say, "You are creating a monster, young lady." His words went in one ear and out the other. I saw a woman with whom I wanted to shower all my affections. If her ego needed stroking, I would do it. I didn't know that the more I did it, the more it was expected.

My Queen became her alter ego's name, and a third-person persona developed. This created a problem in moments where ego stroking was what she desired, and I didn't oblige. Her father's words became clear as we continued to have an issue because she felt that as the primary breadwinner, she was afforded an automatic exemption from remembering birthdays and anniversaries. Every year, she forgets my birthday and her reigning excuse, attention deficit disorder. Initially, that was a joke. Now it's an irritation. Her apologies come bearing gifts from her favorite store, Walmart. Really? Walmart That joke was funny only once. I wouldn't say I like Walmart. Yet, she continues to do it in her disconnection from anything that matters to me.

After a couple of years of sucking it up, I finally told her I was having thoughts of being with other people. It wasn't true. I thought maybe she would be a little jealous. It didn't work. Then I tried to explain the difference between giving someone what they wanted versus what you want them to have by saying, "I love flowers. If I ask you to give me flowers and buy me a car, I may like the car, but I love flowers." I said.

"I understand," she would say. Her typical response meant she didn't want to discuss it any further. She can be very dismissive, and I knew this by watching her with other people. I still chose to be with her because I didn't see it as a big deal. Until it was directed at me. My disappointments are not her fault, but damn I want her to take some responsibility. That is not happening. I am still waiting for those flowers.

My dad told me, "Never make assumptions because it makes an ass of you and me."With My Queen, I made plenty that proved the relevancy of that statement over and over again. It's amazing the things that come back and bite you in the arse For instance, I assumed we shared the same belief in relationships because of where we were born. My Queen was born in the Midwest, but her family is from Alabama. I was born and raised in Lumberton, North Carolina but she fought against religion and I looked for it.

Lumberton, where I'm from, is so tiny, you could miss it if you blink. She said her town was so small you could yell at one end and hear it at the other. We both experienced the 'everybody knows your name and your business' syndrome. In Lumberton, the hang-out spot was a hotel in the center of town. On any night, you could find bikers, skinheads, rappers, line dancers, and bridge clubs all partying together. My Queen recalled the same situation, but here is where things changed, and I missed the significance. I grew up with both parents and matriculated through my formative years in the same town.

My parents fought often but managed to stay together. My Queen's father moved her to Chicago after her mother abandoned them for a married man with empty promises. She spent her summers with her paternal grandmother until she was thirteen. Her father remarried a school teacher at that point, and she relocated permanently to Chicago. Her stepmother enrolled her in all roads leading to law school. My Queen never made it to law school, but she has become a household name. Her stepmom played a massive role in everything, but she refused to acknowledge her. My Queen has never gotten over the split between her parents.

Leaving Lumberton was the obvious next step after high school. My youth had its share of challenges, but I see them as things that have molded me. I appreciate every aspect of it. My Queen refuses to remember her past or people for their role in shaping her future, and she sees it all as the result of her perseverance and determination.

Aside from the parental differences, our coming together on paper is a good match. However, it would have been considered a crime had we met when I was 17. She is ten years my senior. The relationship began as an innocent trip to her house for dinner. She busted me for consistently falling asleep in her class one day. She refused to listen when I tried to explain and put me out of the course. The next day, I went to her office to apologize. She was on a call so I waited outside the door. She glanced up at me and waved me in. " I see." She said looking in my direction. "Thank you," She motioned for me to come in. "Appears my class is not the only class you can't stay awake for. That was Professor Cuffey."

"You checking up on me?"I said slightly irritated and intrigued.

"Never mind that. Why are you sleeping in your classes?"

" I, I, I don't know, " I said which was true. Pro. C was not letting that be an answer. She stood with arms folded, " I'm waiting," she said.

"I don't, well, maybe...

"Take your time."

37

I gathered my nerves before speaking. "I'm not eating enough and I'm borderline diabetic. When I don't eat I get a little lethargic."

"Why are you not eating enough?" She said.

I hesitated for a moment contemplating if I should tell her the truth. Looking at her face I knew she would keep asking until came clean.

"My scholarship only covers school," I said. "And I can't ask my mom for any more help. She's already stretching her money to take care of the family since my dad died."

"Why don't you apply for work-study?" She asked.

"I was going to do it but I missed the deadline?"

"Would you like to be my TA ?" She said.

"Are you serious? I missed the deadline."

Pro. C ignored my comment and handed me a piece of paper. "Here is my address. Come over on Friday night around 7."Our hands touched briefly, and for the first time, we made real eye contact.

Is it me, or is the professor flirting with me? I wondered. At any rate, I wouldn't be able to make it on Friday. "I kinda have plans already," I said.

She took the paper with her address out of my hands.

"I guess you don't need money."

I took it back. "Yes, I do. I misunderstood."I said.

"Okay, come over on Friday. I'll bring you up to speed with all my classes."

Pro. C is short for Professor Cheryl Williams, but mainly because she is a cutie. Hands down the hottest professor on campus, male or female. Everybody wanted to be her TA. Rumor had it that she was a lesbian, but no one could ever get close enough to find out. My friends are going to hate me.

"Thank you so much. I appreciate it."

"You can thank me later. I was once where you are, but that is a story for another time."

I was right. She was feeling me. Before the end of the semester, she was my Queen. I had only dated men before her. There was one time I fantasized about a woman named Bunny. My mom and the other women in Lumberton called her Funny Bunny. It took me a while before I learned that being funny meant being gay.

Bunny rode motorcycles with an all-male bike club. They did not exclude women, but only men rode bikes back home. The women would be perched on the back as eye candy, if at all. Bunny's eye candy's name was Teresa. The men allowed them in because they secretly thought they could turn them. Bunny was more muscular than most men in a sexy, soft way. She and Teresa were both very much

39

feminine.

At least to me, they were. My mother and the other women around town felt differently. Looking back, I think the women were just a little bit jealous. After all, Bunny and Teresa were hot chicks hanging out with their men while home taking care of the children.

My professor, My Queen, reminds me of Bunny. She's older but looks younger than her years. When we connected, she was working out, cycling for charity once a year, and indulging in martial arts. Her body was in fantastic shape. That, like intimacy, went out the window with her obsession with making money.

In the beginning, we spent every moment, not in the classroom, doing something adventurous. Some days we would lie in bed looking at each other and making plans for our future together. She slept on the side closest to the window, and the sun would hit her body perfectly. I marveled at her beauty, and my staring made her uncomfortable. So I stopped. As time moved on the things she disliked began stacking up against my fluid personality. I made it work even giving up an internship with a large law firm to work for her consulting business. It was fun in the beginning. I learned a lot from watching her focus on her two big goals: making lots of money and being on the floor of Congress. My Queen tours the country speaking on restructuring the educational system. She's a charismatic speaker, passionate, and experienced in motivating people to change.

We agreed that I would work for her temporarily. I loved the idea of traveling and spending more time together. She saw it as a way to save money. I saw it as an opportunity to enjoy new places and work on our intimacy. We have been to some of the most romantic places on earth and she turned them into business trips. Sex is a routine experience with no spontaneity. Oh well, she pays the bills so I sucked it up.

After a few months on the road, we were close to her hometown. I had been begging to meet her family so she finally agreed we would take a few days to do that. She was excited to introduce me see her bestie from college, Darrell. He taught her how to ride her first motorcycle. The highlight would be her taking me for a spin on his motorcycle. She sold hers before we met. She promised me she would ride again because I wanted us to have that experience like me being the Teresa to her Bunny. Things quickly changed once we got there. Darrell has two motorcycles, GSX-R 750 and a C50. She felt it would be best for me to ride with him since it had been a while for her— legitimate excuse. I was disappointed, but I sucked it up.

We stopped for a bite at Hard Rock Café. Darrell talked

nonstop about how they became best friends and how he taught her to ride motorcycles and take a spill with grace. I got a kick out of seeing my queen relax. She let her guard down with him as she had never done with me. At one point, he started talking about a trip to Jamaica; they had taken together. I knew she had gone once, but she never mentioned Darrell going with her. He talked about lots of drinking and a ménage. I almost spit out my Diet Coke. She told me it was her and her girlfriend and some random guy. She had given me graphic details while we role-played in one of our early sexual encounters. Darrell was recanting the details of the same scenario, except he was the guy in his version. When I looked surprised, she insisted she had told me it was Darrell. I knew there was no chance I had missed a detail like that. I let her off the hook, quickly dismissing it as maybe my mistake.

Wind in my face again as we rode around town. I was in shock that she had left out that bit of detail. What was going on with them? She knew I had no problem with anything she had done before me. I had to admit I was turned on by it. Now I can put a face to the man that turned My Queen out. And he is not just any man. He is a big sexy dark chocolate Hershey bar with nuts. He reminds me of the Rock, in stature, and how his brow raises when he speaks. His eyes are so black they look midnight blue.

Holding on to him I felt myself getting tingly. My vagina was pressing against the guy that enjoyed My Queen's body just as I do many times. When we came to a stoplight, I scooted as far back as possible. The breeze passed through us, and I felt the wetness of my underwear. Okay, I said to myself as he hit the throttle, bringing my body back into contact with his.

We finally arrive at his place; I immediately head to the bathroom. My Queen announces she has a conference call she forgot she had scheduled. Oh boy, here we go. She had a hard time maintaining a signal in the house. Darrell suggested she go to Starbucks, which was only a few miles away. She could even take a bike for more accessible parking.

"Sounds good. Baby, you ready to ride me now?"

"I don't know if I'm ready just yet." She said. "Awe, Cheryl, you can handle it," Darrell said. "India, baby, I would rather ride around a little more before putting you on with me."

Darrell looks at me. I am about to make one last effort at getting her to change her mind when she says, "India, I'd rather be safe than sorry."

"You're right, baby. Be careful."

She gives me a victory kiss. "I'll be right back." She said rushing out the door.

My only thought was this was the first time meeting her best friend who has been flirting with me and she leaves me alone with him. The same guy I just discovered you let penetrate you. And let's not mention he is so fine he should be wine. What the hell?

Darrell was a very gracious host. We talked about sports and played Street Racer. My mind drifted several times as I watched him handle the joystick. The quick tension in his face, slowly releasing in a smile, was orgasmic. My Kegel's muscle was holding back an eruption. I was mentally undressing him and our eyes locked. Damn, he caught me, I said to myself. Oh no, he's probably reading my mind too. Feeling tremendously embarrassed, I stand up.

"Where is the bathroom?" I blurted out.

He chuckled and motioned toward the bathroom. "In the same place, it was the last time you used it."

I ran past him to the bathroom. Staring in the mirror I felt guilty. I knew I wasn't able to hide things. So he knew I was attracted to him. Yet I love my Queen. Yeah, things are rough but I need to get my hormones together. Darrell's knock startled me.

"Are you okay?"

"I'm good. I'll be out in a minute." I said going back to the mirror for answers. What's going on with me? Go back in there and be calm.

I opened the door as Darrell is walking away. I started walking out as he turned back. We collided with one another. He backed me up to the wall placing a hand on the wall next to my head. His face was close to mine I felt his breath and body heat. He broke the silence

"My toilet seat shifts sometimes. I wanted to make sure you didn't fall in".

"I had to clean my contacts." I said with a girlish giggle. Lying my ass off. I wasn't wearing contacts. "You know, um, they dry out when I get heated. I mean when they get heated." Darrel laughed knowingly. Neither one of us moved for what seemed like an eternity. The heat between us began to rise as he leaned in closer. Our lips almost touching. I closed my eyes just as my cell phone rang. I slowly opened them and looked at my phone.

"All day without a signal..." I said holding up my phone so he could see it. "It's my Queen."

"Saved by the bell," Darrell whispers as I move away from him to answer the call. He goes to the kitchen. I took a couple of deep breaths as I watched him walk away.

"Hey, bae. I'm good…See ya soon. You too."

"That was my Queen, she's on her way back," I said yelling toward the kitchen.

"I'm having a beer. Do you want one?"

"None for me. Too many calories" I said.

"Awe, come on. I have wine too if that's more your thing. No pressure."

No pressure? Everything felt like pressure to me. Just being near him felt like pressure.

"Well, I guess one glass is allowed." I caved.

"Red or white?"

Before I could say red, he handed me a wine glass and was about to pour in some red.

"What if I had said white?"

"You don't like white."

"How did you know that?"

"I heard you say it earlier."

Wow! It took My Queen months to remember that and occasionally she will come home with Moscato.

"Cheers."

"Cheers."

I gulped down the wine and extended my hand for a refill. Darrell took the glass and kissed me. I pushed him back. He looked shocked and started to apologize. I interrupted him and leaped into his arms, locking my legs around him and kissing him so passionately that I almost broke a tooth. He pinned me to the wall I could feel every inch of his penis through our clothes. Slowly he walked me to the sofa and placed me down getting on his knees. Our eyes stayed locked and he parted my legs. He searched my face for assurance before asking."Are you okay?"

I nodded, " Yes."

Darrell cupped my face and paused, still searching my eyes. I gave it to him and allowed my head to fall back closing my eyes. The fire inside of me intensifies. I look at him as he goes down closer to my vagina and looks up at me. I try to turn away. He quickly turns me back towards him.

"Oh shit! I'm in trouble now."

In Plain Sight

S AMANTHA.

If you were born in the US, you have probably played hide and seek at least a dozen times. There are variations but the premise is the same. Players run and hide while the person who has been unlucky to be "it" counts, "1,2,3,4,5,6,7,8,9,10, ready or not, here I come." And then starts searching for them. The other players stay hidden until it looks safe to try to run to home base. If you are the unfortunate one to get caught, you are now "it".

That game and my cousin Chantelle changed the course of my life. One day, I was about 9 or 10, we were playing and Chantelle's brother Kevin was it. Even though he was smaller than most of us, he was the fastest. I hid behind the giant weeping willow tree in Big Momma's front yard on a hill. It was perfect for hiding because the trunk was big enough for three people to hide and nothing around it to obstruct the view of Kevin. I was the only one that ever went out that far though. I stood in plain sight, and no one could see me. The possibility of being exposed is a turn-on. The " it " person had to risk everyone getting to base before them if they came out that far to find them. Kevin was fast, but even he did not venture out that far.

As soon as I saw Kevin dart around the house in the opposite direction, I took off. Running as fast as I could to home base. Chantelle and I met up at the same time. He tagged her, missing me, and kept going after the rest of the kids, Chantelle grabbed my arm and

started pulling me, "Come here, real quick, let me show you something." We were heading toward the shed that Big Momma said was off-limits.

"Oh no, I protested, I'm not going in there."

"Hush," she said still dragging me. "We have to hurry up."

Before I could protest more, Chantelle pulled me into the darkness of the shed with little streaks of light filtering through the cracked boards.

"Look at what I found," she said handing me a magazine, The naked woman on the cover intrigued me. On the inside were naked men and women. I was thumbing threw the pages when I saw pictures of men with women and women with women in different sexual positions. "We're not supposed to be in here looking at this stuff," I said still looking through the pages.

"Hush, someone will hear you."

"Have you done anything like this before?" I whispered.

"No," she said. "Do you want to?" I knew what she meant but I was only thinking about the tingling in my cooch. It felt like I had to pee.

"Did you hear me, Sam? Do you wanna try this?" Chantelle pointed to the image of two women touching each other's vagina. While outside, the game was almost over.

"What if we get caught?" I said.

"We won't. I hide in here all the time. Nobody comes in here. It's scary. Just keep your voice down."

She wasn't wrong. The shed had holes in it to allow all types of vermin access to our families' heirlooms, furniture, and charity or the dump. There were hundreds of sexually explicit magazines in a crate.

My Uncle Chester probably owned them. I heard my dad and mom laughing one time about him being addicted to sex. He was a little creepy. All of us kids hated it when he bounced us on his knee. With the girls, he would sometimes touch our budding breasts or butts and act like it was an accident. Uncle Chester was also caught "messing with" one of my cousins who was only 17 at the time. The family blamed her for being "fast and frisky" and never chastised his behavior at all. However, after that incident, Auntie Ann never let us sit on his lap anymore. She would shoo us away like we were the problem. Chantelle snapped me out of my thoughts when I noticed she had pulled her shorts and panties down. "Hurry up," she said helping me with mine.

While we were standing butt-ass naked Chantelle pulled me closer to her until her pelvic area was pressing against mine. When I felt the warmth of her vagina I pushed her away. She raised her shirt revealing two huge breasts. I wasn't nursed as a baby but I wanted to be nursed by Chantelle. My body went stiff.

"Do you want to kiss one?" she asked.

Yes, I nodded, and thus began my quest for sexual exploration.

I visited that shed a lot looking at those magazines. I fantasized about doing everything I saw. It looked interesting. I wanted to try things with Chantelle.

"That stuff is for white people, " she argued. "Do you see any black people in any of those pictures?"

"So what? Maybe I'll be the first."

"Not with me." She protested.

The next time we were in the shed, I didn't care about her saying no before. I lifted her skirt and put a finger inside her coochie. She let me do it for a while then she pushed my hand away.

"Stop it. I don't know where your hands have been."

"Stop playing. I washed my hands."

"Did it feel good though?" I asked.

"It doesn't matter. Your hands are dirty."

"They are now," I said putting my fingers in her face. She tried to squeeze past me, but the shed was overflowing with stuff. There was nowhere for her to go. I went under her skirt again.

"I know you liked it. Open your legs wider." I said fingering her until her juices ran down my hand.

Chantelle was turned out. I loved to kiss. Chantelle was a very basic kisser and became a drag after a while. I started inviting other cousins and friends to the shed. Her best friend, Simone wanted to do it all the time. She was more fun than Chantelle but she couldn't kiss. I cut her off. That made her mad. She stalked the shed and threw rocks at the door when she thought I was in there. That only boosted my already inflated ego. Chantelle was happy I kicked Simone to the curb. They got into a heated argument and Simone promised her she would get even.

The shed was the spot for a long time, but all good things end. Even though I was tired of Chantelle, the sex was good once she let me do what I wanted and she tried new things. We agreed to do it only one more time. It started cool. I had set up one of the beds and would bring sheets and a blanket, so we had the option to lie down. We were completely naked and kissing when Auntie Anne, Chantelle's mom, burst through the door. Chantelle got a whipping because she was the oldest. In between licks, Auntie Anne would say, "Girls don't do that with girls. It's a sin against God. God will get you if you sin."

I don't know how Auntie Anne found out, but I have suspicions. Simone's face was the first face I saw when we came out. I learned three things that day: never get caught with your pants down with a girl, never piss off someone you are doing the nasty with, and according to Auntie's God, sex with girls is a sin, especially if it's your cousin.

My family built the church so on some level they felt like they owned it. I suppressed my feelings for females for a long time. I believed I would go to hell almost all my adult life because I liked being with girls.

To this day, Chantelle averts eye contact with me at family functions. I live my life wide open, but it's scary. I've been blessed to hear everything my family says about me in small doses. Otherwise, I may have stayed in the closet much longer. The things people said were harsh. I've known people who have committed suicide because of words. My other coochie-bumping cousins and Simone live under the principles of our upbringing in the church. Nothing wrong with that, but they are married to men who cheat or otherwise abuse them, and they pretend to be happy while they steadily gain weight. If it's not the food they are addicted to, it's Jesus or both.

THE BODY KNOWS THE SCORE

James Ruffin was my first official encounter with a male. I was twelve, and he was sixteen. His mother married my uncle. I did not have a type when it came to guys, but I knew what being aroused felt like. I didn't like James because he teased and picked on me. He called me Earl Campbell because I have big thighs. I was very thick for my age, and I hated being teased. James did it non-stop. I learned later that he was teasing me because he liked me. It surprised me when he slid behind me in bed as we all slept over at Big Mommas after her Friday social.

Big Momma's house was the place to be on a Friday night. Our parents would play cards and drink liquor. All of us kids would run in and out of the house playing. They didn't care as long as nobody started crying or Big Momma didn't get tired of the door slamming. The only time we had issues was if James started picking on us. He was much older and kind of a bully back then(More on him later).

I dreaded any type of conflict because my daddy was very stern and a master disciplinarian. If one of the other kids did something, he made me sit with the adults. He didn't care who started it. I made it a point to keep the peace among the kids. We didn't get into any big trouble for real.

Most of the time, we played hide and go seek, board games, or watched television. A few of us budding alcoholics sneaked sips of the liquor and half-empty beer cans. It was easy to tell which kid drank the most. They would sleep before everybody else. At the end of the night, our parents would have to prove to Big Momma they were sober enough to drive home, much less take us, children, with them.

Big Momma would say, "Leave them children be." Daddy never wanted me out of his sight. He would insist on taking me home no matter how late it was. Big Momma loved my daddy. He was a charming man. That's how he got my mom and all of the other women he never quite let go of after he married my mom. However, that night, my daddy's charm was not enough. Big Momma put her foot down. Everyone had been drinking way too much for her comfort.

"That girl will sleep back there with the rest of the kids. Pick her up in the morning." She told my daddy. He kissed me good night, and Big Momma had her way.

I hadn't entirely fallen back asleep when James slid in behind me. I pretended to be asleep. I knew it was James because his old spice arrived before he did. His penis was poking me in my butt crack. He inched my panties over to the side with his penis. I felt a twinge in my coochie. I pretended to be stretching and moving so my panties loosened. It kinda felt good. He didn't penetrate me or anything like that. I let him play for a minute and then I bumped him to the floor.

That was my first lesson in the body's ability to become aroused even when you are not attracted to the person. If someone touches you in a certain way, you will respond. I realized I also liked how the male body felt against mine.

Since then or before, I'm not sure. I've grown to love having sex all the time. It's right up there with breathing. The human body is the most excitingly fantastic thing in the world. If I could have sex with everyone who has ever aroused me, my life would be much more fulfilled. Instead, I masturbate in vivid colors, so I sometimes feel what he and she experience during the same session.

AFFINITY FOR FEMALES

Getting married to a man was always in the cards for me. There were too many roadblocks to being gay, even though I adore being with a woman and everything she brings. It's not the same for me as I'm with a man. I don't identify with the term bisexual because it doesn't capture all of who I am with men and women. It frustrates me when people try to lump them together based on sex. I find pleasure in them both equally and in distinctly different ways.

Freddie was the love of my life. We met at the first job I ever had. He was the back-line cook, and I was a cashier. My appetite for sex fed his hunger. His eagerness to explore matched mine. I wanted him for the rest of my life.

Six months into the marriage, sex with him became predictable. I waited for Freddie to bring the spice equal to mine. He would go for a while, but it got old quickly. Freddie couldn't keep up with my expanding appetite. I tried to coach him, saying, "Freddie, can we mix it up instead of doing new stuff until it becomes old?"

"What are you talking about, Samantha? We do stuff."

"Yeah, but then we do it to death. Can we do new stuff mixed with old while finding newer stuff to do?"

"Like what?"

"Forget it." I would say that after several rounds of saying the same thing differently. It was exhausting.

He tried to do as I asked but was back to the routine. I would complain, masturbate, and ignore it until I finally had enough.

"Freddie, we have to mix it up."

"I thought we were." He replied.

"Tie me up and gag me. Do something different."

"What's up with the violence?"

"That is kinky, not violent."

"I want to try new stuff, but you like to take shit too far sometimes."

"Like when?"

"Like when you asked me if you could put your black thumb thing in my ass."

"I heard it was a turn-on for straight guys who wanted explosive nuts. But that's not the point; I want you to initiate new positions and maybe even some toys."

"I don't need toys. I need you to decide on things sometimes. The toys I want to be used on me. Just forget it." I yelled.

"Oh, come on, and lay down." He said, hugging me with his usual groping of my ass.

"You see what I mean?" I shouted.

"I'm confused. You wanted me to take control." Freddie said.

"Not control, initiative, and I want you to enjoy it. Don't do it because I asked you to."

"You are making no sense." He said totally confused.

Freddie had no clue what I was talking about. He was the middle child of five and the only male. He was used to being told what to do. I wanted him to come up with ideas on his own. Freddie still was not getting the concept of what I needed. The more I showed him how to make love to me, the more I wanted to make love to someone I could give the feeling I longed for.

I went to the left. Freddie knew I liked women in the beginning. He was not concerned about it too much because Freddie felt no woman could ever give him what he could. I rationalized finding a woman based on that and being with a woman was not the same as being with another man. I rationalized that as not the same as cheating. Intellectually, I knew that was bullshit, but I made myself okay with it. I wouldn't be able to do it if I allowed myself to see it any other way. I drank the monogamy Kool-aid when I said, "I do." I could stay true to it, but I had not factored in things changing.

Marlene was a game-changer. She was a gorgeous white chocolate sister. I noticed her flashy double D's, classy attitude, ghetto booty, and business savvy. Marlene could not be missed if you tried. However, I didn't think she was remotely interested in women. Our bond was not one where we shared everything, but everyone knew Marlene only talked about men and that she wanted desperately to have the storybook wedding. We were the only black female team leader in the entire plant. Sticking together was imperative to surviving the environment; we usually talked about that over lunch. We were grabbing a bite when Marlene caught me by surprise.

"Have you ever had sex with a woman?" She said as I was taking a bite out of my sandwich. I held off my shock. This may be a trick to get me fired, so I called her out.

"Is that an offer?" I said.

Marlene said no, but her giggle sounded yes.

"I saw you and Gabrielle walking out of the restroom and...?"

She paused, searching for words. I interrupted her thoughts.

"What are you implying?"

"Have you had sex with Gabrielle?"

"In the bathroom?"

"I'm not asking if you did it in the bathroom. You knew what I meant. Why are you being difficult?"

Marlene was shifting her weight from side to side in her chair, which told me her vagina was blushing too. I watched her squirm and tried to carry on the conversation expressionless.

"I saw you are coming out of the bathroom with Gabrielle, and the thought crossed my mind."

"What?"

"Gabrielle is a lesbian, and nobody knew at first. So I thought maybe you were hiding too."

"Odd thing to just pop into someone's head...don't you think?"

"I'm just going to say it. I want you to show me what it's like to be with a woman."

My face turned beet red. "Are you for real?" I said.

"I know it sounds crazy."

"Wow. You just asked me to have sex with you over lunch."

"I'm curious, and this is a good time for me to explore since I'm single."

"I'm married. Remember?"

"I know that."

"Oh, I forgot, you like them married and unavailable. Speaking of marriage, what happened to your sugar daddy?"

"His wife happened."

"What?"

"She found out and confronted me at my house."

"How did she know where you lived?"

"He told her."

"What?"

"This idiot told his wife that he was in love with me and wanted a divorce. She wanted to meet the woman taking him away from his family."

"He gave her your address?"

"He said it was for the sake of his son."

"Whoa, that's scary."

"That's crazy. She could have done anything to me, but all she wanted to do was to tell me to let him go.

First, she asked me if I loved him. I told her no. Then, she asked me to back off."

"That is bizarre."

"The crazy part is she asked if I gave him head, how often, and did he eat me?"

"Shut the front door. Did you tell her?"

"I did. As desperate as she was to come to me and ask, I was equally willing to give her all she needed to keep him away from me."

"Girl, you are too much."

"I'm just over all of that type of drama. Let's get back to you and me." She said with almost a commanding tone as if reliving that moment boosted her confidence in this one.

"Oh, I get it," I said. "Now that you have kicked big daddy to the curb, you thought you would try a woman?"

"I want you. Not just any woman," Her words made me blush. I covered my face to hide my cheeks. My fair skin would indeed have given me away.

"Marlene, who does that?" I said, trying to recover.

"Will you please stop asking the questions and supplying the answers in the same sentence?"

"Hold on, sister. You came to me. Pardon me for wanting to know more about why you want to have sex with me."

"I've been attracted to you for a long time. I'm not trying to be a lesbian. I want to explore all parts of my sexuality, which has been on my mind since I was a kid."

"Why didn't you ask Gabrielle?"

"I'm not attracted to Gabrielle."

My coochie started blushing, thinking about my face between those double D's. We are about the same build, but her breasts are enormous. Realizing a hottie was pursuing me, I had to put her to the test to see if she was sincere about wanting to get with me.

"Okay, before I take the assignment, we have to kiss."

In the middle of the restaurant, Marlene walked over to me and kissed me as I had never had a woman do before. I shouted. "Sold." Marlene started beaming.

"When do I start?" I said.

Classes began immediately. I invited Marlene to our home as often as she was available. We had sex in various places in the house. Never in the bed Freddie and I shared. The kids called her Auntie. Freddie liked her coming around. I seemed happier. He had no clue about the depth of his perception. He decided to play Cupid and hooked Marlene up with his frat brother, Randy. I protested. Randy is a player. Marlene wanted something permanent. Right now, I was it, and I was not particularly eager to share.

That was the beginning of the end of my relationship with Marlene. Randy was all over her. He gave her the attention she craved, and then he popped the question. Marlene would still get with me, but we began having discussions of marriage and religion at work. Eventually, she quoted scriptures denouncing same-sex relationships. I drew the line once she started repenting after we had sex.

Refocusing my attention on my marriage, I started noticing Freddie was never home. He worked nights, and I worked days. He slept or hung out with his frat brothers when he was home. I wanted more sex. Marlene had been a distraction. With her out of the picture, the void returned. The time I had with Freddie and Marlene helped me understand what I desired, and there was no turning back. Maybe I could eventually convert Freddie to the idea of me having a girlfriend, also.

Where do I go from here? There have to be some others like me. Searching the internet, I found a bisexual meet-up scheduled for the following week. It appeared to be a support group. I went to the first meet-up last night and ran into Gabrielle and her girlfriend. It is about to get very interesting.

JUSTICE UNPLUGGED

I knew my girl was a liar when I caught her kissing the dog. "Honey, I didn't know you felt so strongly about it." She said. I promise I won't do it again. Then she kissed me on the nose. I had no idea she was an addict. She has what's called EPL (extreme pet lover) syndrome. People who suffer from it will kiss their pets and pet their partners.

I believed my girl desired to make me happy, but the pull was much too strong. She signed up for PLA (Pet Lovers Anonymous). I went with her a few times. Going to PLA helped me understand her better, and I embraced the possibility of letting her kiss me as long as she washed her face before she kissed me. I thought we were getting closer. We were excellent for a while, but the separation from the dog was getting to her. She started distancing herself from me. My reliance upon her for kisses and affection took over me. Maybe if I backed up off the dog and made advances at her more, she would get the hint.

After a few days of her being on the road, I planned a midnight rendezvous to seduce her. The candles were lit. Maxwell and Musiq Soulchild were in the CD player. The wine was in the glass, and the bubble bath was warm. Not an original plan, but I wanted to get between their thighs. This trick tells me she is too tired. I heard a ringing in my ear and the familiar sound of a cheater in the house. Without her permission or any prior warning, I read her cell phone records and her credit card spending and finally confronted her.

"How dare you violate my privacy"

"Trick is that all you got"

"This is why things are not going to work for us?"

"No, this is why things haven't worked for us. You don't know how to own your shit."

I admitted I was wrong. She took the victim route. I was willing to overlook the dog, the three-hour rides to "clear her head," and the lies about being out of town. But, I drew the line at no sex. She had checked out of our relationship long before. It hurt, but the funny thing is that I still wanted to try. To think we were together for two years. I wonder how many times I kissed that damn dog without knowing it.

A lie at its core is truth. When someone lies, their goal is to achieve an outcome more desirable than what will happen without it. The African American Bisexual woman lies to protect her family, job, safety, or values. In some cases, all of those concerns apply.

Lying about her sexuality indefinitely is possible, but she will get to a point where she no longer desires to live that way. If she doesn't own it outright, she gets caught in some compromising situation that forces her hand.

Lying for extended periods creates a backlog of resentment and holds her hostage to her fears. Coming clean gives her a quantum leap into the Art of Selfishness, the final frontier of unconditional love. Her fears may take over if she doesn't leap, and she assimilates into the heterosexual or homosexual community. Assimilation invokes her ability to practice the art of Social Networking.

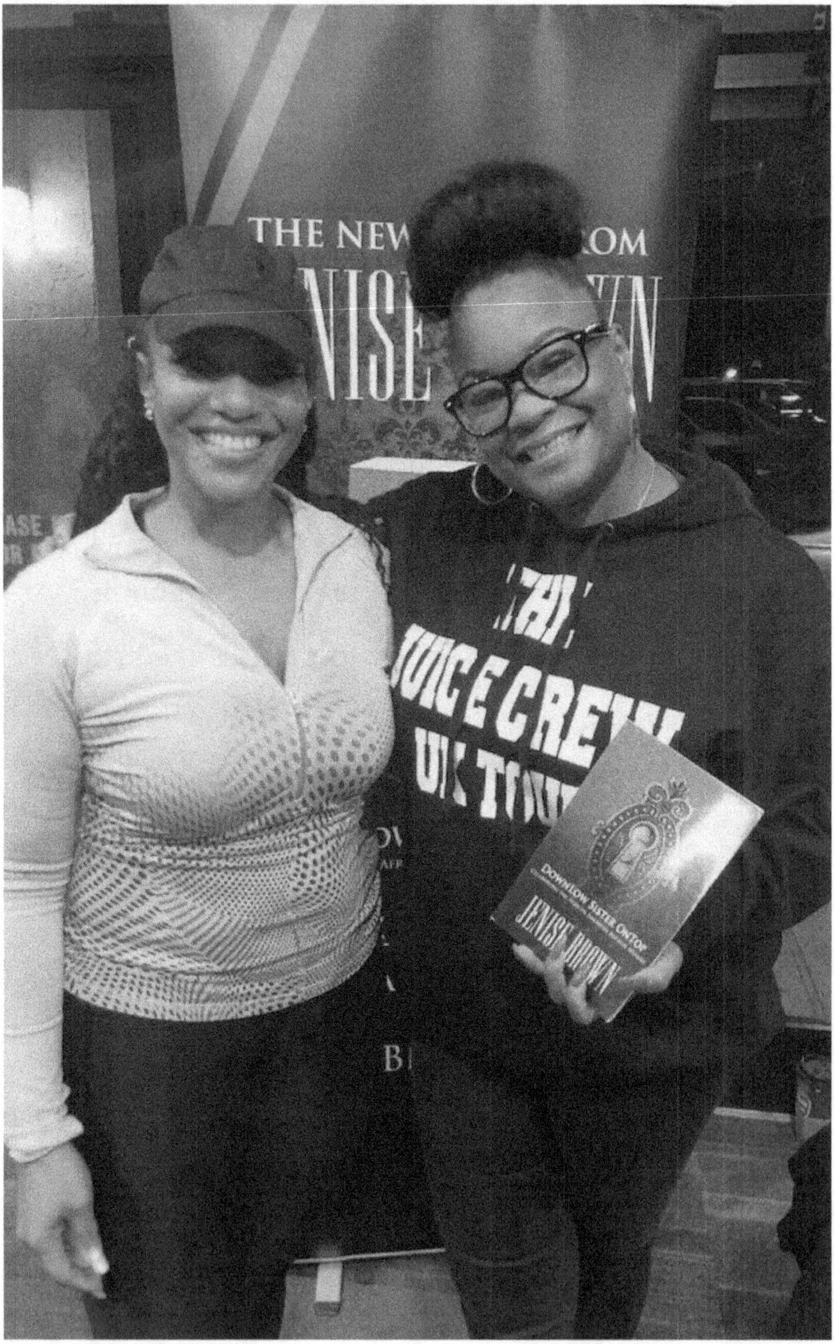
DownLow Sister OnTop
JENISE BROWN

The Art of Social Networking

TO COMBINE OR MIX SO THAT THE
CONSTITUENT PARTS ARE
INDISTINGUISHABLE FROM ONE
ANOTHER; TO BLEND TO CREATE
SOMETHING NEW
To promote bisexuals aiding justice around
the world

Statistically speaking, lesbians and 'heterosexual' men have at least one thing in common. They both have a fear of competition and feelings of inadequacy if their partner has a relationship with someone who is of the opposite sex. In other words, if two women are together, reports say one feels more threatened when the other chooses a satellite relationship (a relationship outside of the two) with a man versus a satellite relationship with a woman. Some bisexuals have evolved into establishing rules of non-monogamy or adopting polygamy because they understand that pursuing happiness is not linear. The African American bisexual woman can love either sexual orientation; therefore, the competitive edge related to gender generally does not exist for her. She appreciates what each exposure brings to the table and understands that one is not a replacement for or beats the other.

I'm Healthy Because I'm Sick

ZOE.

I was confused about my sexuality in my youth. There was no one like me to whom I could turn. I didn't understand why I simultaneously liked to dress like a guy and a girl. I knew I was bisexual but didn't know what to call it.

There were plenty of examples of what gay looked like. My Aunt Terri was a lesbian. She was Uncle Terry at first. Then he had a sex change operation and became Aunt Terri. It took me a while to understand why he went through all that to still prefer dating women. I thought it was crazy at the time. After many conversations, I got it. Aunt Terri is a lesbian born into a male body. It's like wearing a pair of shoes because they fit but preferring boots because they reflect your style. We identify with what feels right.

My parents prayed over me to exorcise the demon. We had bottles of holy water in every room of the house. Grammy lived with us too. She carried a bottle in her bosom. She would throw it on me at the oddest times. One day I was on the toilet, and here comes Grammy tossing holy water on me and speaking in tongues. I wanted to tell them that they were going to hell, but where I come from, you respect your elders even if they are wrong. So, instead, my parents did something that, as a kid, hurt more. They ignored me. There were times I felt like disappearing. Instead, I became a therapist.

The female body turns me on more than the male. As a youth, I fantasized about being in a dark room surrounded by nothing but women. In the darkness, I would touch and feel all the different breasts and butts, and vaginas. It would take forever for me to pick one I liked. When I fantasized about men, it was only two men; the difference was that I only wanted the one with the chiseled body. I love strong arms and a big penis. The light would come on in both instances, and everybody would disappear. That's how life looked to me in this body.

True story...I had a crush on this girl named Brianna. She was into guys but flirted with me hard when no one looked. I dressed most days very androgynously but beefed up my stud look for her. One day I was walking down the hall, and Brianna was coming toward me. I threw her a head nod and grabbed my crotch.

"Why are you doing that, you freak? You look stupid."

Everybody, including the teachers, laughed at what

she said. I felt like I was going to melt into the floor. I played it off and kept walking right out of the school. I cried all the way home. Late that night, I had an epiphany. It was stupid, but I got her attention in front of everybody. Cool. The next day I walked around the halls strutting in a tight sweater and fitted jeans that showed off my curvy body to show them I am many things. You may not like it, but you will see me.

Brianna and I hooked up eventually, but she was sleeping with most of the football team. She got pregnant by one of them, and things got messy. We remained friends, but I couldn't deal with all her extra. Around the same time, all of that was going down, and my brother's friend Carlos was trying to get with me. He is older by two years and was already in college. I had a crush on him that dated back to when I was six. He was the body in my fantasies. No longer six and looking sexy, he was on me whenever he came home. My brother didn't like it. I went out with him anyway. We dated for several years off and on. He was my steady guy, and I found different girls online. That's where I met Sophie.

My parents spent many dollars in therapy trying to get my queerness corrected. Therapy helped me figure out how to be queer. Ironically, I counsel lesbian-identified women who date men. It's a volunteer job for the local LGBT youth center, but my core practice includes women and men of every orientation.

At the center, the term youth refers to anyone aged 18 to 35. There is a huge gap in age because being out of the closet' or existing in what I call an unconventional lifestyle does not sometimes happen until well beyond the age of thirty. The pressure to come out or not as lesbian, gay, bi, trans, et cetera can be an overwhelmingly long and challenging process because the individual has to own it first. Without assistance from others who have come through it or anyone willing to support them, non-heterosexuals or non-conformists may find it too painful to acknowledge their uniqueness.

The work others, like myself, do in this area has helped to shorten that time. It's a rewarding career. I witness transformation at its best. My prized client Kandi was the worst case of identity crisis I have ever encountered. At our first meeting, she was an extremely attractive twenty-six-year-old who cowered a lot and avoided direct eye contact. Everything she wore hid her body. For years she dated men in secret while being involved with bisexual women. Yet, she identified as a lesbian and despised bisexual.

"Doc, it's like this. I can get a man to do anything I want him to do. Look at me."

"Anything like what?" I asked.

"Sex, pay my bills, give me money, or take me on trips. You name it. I can get them to do it."

"Do you enjoy being with them, or is it all business?" I asked.

"It's all business. Don't get me wrong. I've been with some decent guys, but I could never be serious about them."

"Why?"

"Most of them are married and...." Kandi paused. Staring off into space. I didn't want to lose the moment.

"Go on," I said.

"I just could never do that." Kandi took a deep

breath. "I don't want to talk about that anymore."

"Okay, Let's talk about the women you have dated."

"I don't call them that." She said.

"What do you call them?" I asked.

"Ho's mostly." She said.

"Prostitutes?"

"No Doc. I don't pay for shit. These bitches are ho's. Prostitutes are in business to make money. These ho's do it just because. That's why I can't trust none of them."

"Tell me more about the trust, I said. Have you been cheated on?"

"Yes," Kandi's demeanor reflected some sadness.

"Do you want to stop?" I asked.

"No," she said after a long pause. "She was the best thing that had ever happened to me. We hit it off from the start."

"Was she a Ho?"

"She's not a ho. Kandi shouted. She's a lady."

"I apologize. You said she is a lady. Are you still in

touch with her?"

"No," Kandi became solemn once more.

"Are you okay talking about her?"

Kandi paused as if she was reliving a moment. She took another deep breath. "I'm cool."

"Okay, so what happened with you and ...?"

"Danita," she said.

"With you and Danita?"

"It is straightforward. We were planning to have a baby. She found the guy and slept with him. She didn't tell me until after the pregnancy was confirmed."

"She was pregnant after the first try?"

"No, she slept with him several times. She said, Not how we planned it."

Kandi stood up and started pacing. "I loved her and wanted to make it work so I forgave her. But she was in love with him. He didn't want me in the baby's life, so she chose..."Tears began welling up in her eyes.

"She chose him?" I asked

"I want her to be happy. I'm just walking away."Kandi sat back down. " I don't want to talk

DownLow July 29 Thirsty

about her anymore."

"Okay, let's look at your relationship with your Ho's. Have you ever been cheated on by one of your Ho's?"

"Ho's don't cheat, Doc. You are funny." She chuckled.

"Then why can't you trust them."

"They can't settle for one person. They can't be with

one person."

"Studies have compared the level of monogamy amongst orientations. They say that lesbians are the most reported cases of sexual infidelity, followed by heterosexuals, then gay males, and bringing up the rear are the bisexuals."

"So what, those people don't know the ho's I know." She said

"What does being bisexual mean to you?"

"You have sex with men and women at the same time." She said.

"What if I told you the term bisexual is an identity that means being open to loving men and women?"

"Doc, you are too funny. That's what I just said."

"What you said was they have sex with them simultaneously. I said they are capable of loving both at the same time."

Kandi was not happy with my response. Her irritability increased. "Sex and love mean the same thing," she said.

We had found the root of Kandi's confusion and a

starting point for her treatment. She was unaware of the fundamental differences between sex and love; she hated herself. Her abuse of bisexual women and detachment from the men she slept with were all about her hating what she didn't understand about herself.

Kandi loved her ex and found peace with her ex choosing a man. This revealed her capacity to grasp the possibilities of a woman who identifies as lesbian, like herself, choosing to be with a man, which is okay. It breaks the boundaries of what the categories of sexual identity tend to create and make so rigid. Kandi was finally developing an awareness of her freedom to choose without it being right or wrong which is, at its core, a solid foundation to let go of fear, guilt, and shame.

It took several months of intensive reprogramming before Kandi finally began loving herself. She still refuses to use the term bisexual to define herself. She prefers cross-gender loving. Sophie suggested I invite her to Club Beijui.

"Hun, she is not ready for that yet."

"I thought you said she needed to be around more

women like her."

"That's true, but the women in my club are at a different level."

"You are kidding me. Sophie said. I thought you were open to all bisexual black women."

"We are. But the ones who are just getting comfortable with themselves still have to get past the hypocrisy in the world. That takes a little longer considering all the daily barriers they face."

"Exactly why she needs to be there."

"Sophie, Kandi is not ready. When they come to us still fragmented, they can't handle how we roll."

"Exactly how do you roll?" She said fishing for answers she knew I could not give her. What happens at Club Beijui stays at Club Beijui. Members do not discuss it with non-members. That includes significant others.

"This is how we roll." I started tickling her. She hates it when I do that, but I love hearing her laugh, which creates the perfect diversion from her questions. I knew she was only prying because she didn't know what had gone on, and it was killing her. My Sophie is relentless when she wants to know something. She will keep going until she is proven right or wrong.

There was one time she thought I was cheating. It was at a time when my shyness morphed into flirtation. I used to get shy around women in my early years, but men were no problem. We were at a friend's wedding, and she saw me interact with several people.

Sophie told me, "You are only shy around people you're attracted to." I love her, so I tried to watch my behavior, but I think it's true. She made a point of watching me at functions and pointing out things. It drove me nuts. I conceded.

"Baby, you are correct. You may want to switch careers and come to work with me." My attempt at a joke did not go over well. Sophie nearly bit my head off with her response. "I could do your job, but you are the only client I would have time for. Get your shit together."

I tried to laugh it off. She didn't laugh.

"Okay, baby." I knew when enough was enough. I needed her to process it, or she would never let it go. I love her mean ass. We have been together for over five years. I share almost everything with her, even concerning clients, without violating patient confidentiality. She knows my job elicits aggression on occasion. My clients deal with much pinned-up frustration, and I provide a safe place for them to address it. Sometimes it's intense, and as the therapist, I appear to be the antagonist.

It doesn't take some clients long to figure out that I may have experience in the matters they bring to my couch. My androgyny has prompted questions that ended with me firing my clients. If they ask, I answer truthfully within the confines of my person's relevance to their recovery. Most often than not, it ends there, and we move on.

I've only had one person arrested; he was a "straight" guy who had contracted aids from another "straight" guy. I reminded him of the other guy. He hit me. He had been off his meds for a few days. I didn't know it at the time. I subsequently dropped the charges. But Sophie wanted blood. However, that is never her final answer.

Sophie is a girlie girl. Her femininity can be misconstrued as soft and demure. Quite the contrary, Sophie will go to that ass when she feels provoked or threatened. However, she goes through stages with her anger that has fascinated me from the first time I met her. She's adept at getting to a good-feeling place with situations. Many could benefit from her process. She said it was something she picked up studying the teachings of Abraham Hicks and the Law of Attraction. I watched the process at warp speed when I told her my client struck me. She went ballistic.

"We will sue him, his doctors, and anyone who knew he was off his meds," she said immediately.

"Honey, he is one of my pro bono clients."

"Then sue the center. They have liability insurance."

"They didn't know either," I said

"Oh, someone knew. They didn't care." At that moment her eyes narrowed. She took a long deep breath. The switch was happening inside her.

"It is so sad." She said. "Someone lets him walk around like that. That poor guy." Her emphatic side is now in full effect. I couldn't just let her stop there.

"What happened to make him pay, sue him, sue them...?" I chided.

"Zoe, he didn't know what he was doing." And this is the moment she goes too far by wanting to invite someone to dinner or suggest something like taking a client to Club Beijui. I love Sophie's giving spirit, but the club is not an option for Kandi.

There was a time early in our relationship I could talk to Sophie about anything. I think it's time I stop talking to her about work. She's becoming more and more triggered by her past trauma while working in male-dominated fields.

Sophie is a systems analyst. She's one of the best in her company and the only female doing what she does. Her male colleagues are jealous and give her a hard time daily. She can handle her own, so that is not the real issue. A few of the guys constantly hit on her but just enough to where it is not sexual harassment. She loves what she does, and the money is excellent, so she gives them a pass. "As long as they don't touch me, I'm good," she says.

91

There is only one other female in the department, Susan, who happens to be Sophie's direct report. Unfortunately for Sophie, Susan cares very little about girl power. She's sleeping with Justin, the office gigolo. Justin hates the fact that Sophie keeps turning him down.

"No woman ever says no to Justin."

He speaks of himself in the third person. Justin is a good-looking guy, but Sophie loves vaginas… mine, to be exact. His ego makes it hard to take no for an answer. Any woman who refuses him has to be gay.

Justin's borderline disrespect is reaching a boiling point with Sophie. The harassment turned up after seeing me with her at a restaurant. It's hard for me to keep my hands off her, and he witnessed me groping her ass. Justin is a non-factor. He will not cause too much of a problem because he doesn't want Susan to get wind of it. But Sophie has buckled to Justin's pressure and agreed to a date.

"Have you lost your mind, woman?"

"It will get him off my back."

"I think it will be the total opposite effect."

"I don't want a repeat of my last job."

"That was different, Sophie. Justin is not your boss. He can't have you fired."

Her fear stems from an incident at a company Christmas party. Her manager saw us kissing under the mistletoe. Though the company had a policy barring discrimination based on sexual orientation, he saw this as an opportunity to pursue his sexual desires. When Sophie turned him down, he went after her full throttle to get her fired. It almost destroyed her. She and I had only been dating for a short period. I took the risk and counseled her. I do not recommend that, but for her and me, it worked. Her family never knew a thing. You see, Sophie is still in the closet with her family. I think they already know but are waiting for her to tell them. They genuinely have their issues to be concerned with. Her parents are divorcing. Her sister's husband is cheating, and her nephew cross-dresses. I think there is more to her wanting to keep us on the down low.

We pretend to be roommates around them. There is this thing we do call date night with the family. My ex,

Carlos (more on him later), serves in this capacity. For years he has been the go-to guy for family date nights, holidays, and all functions involving the family. To them, I'm the lonely best friend who can't get a date.

Back to Carlos. Sophie and I decided to get pregnant. From a financial standpoint, I needed to get pregnant first. Sophie wants artificial insemination.

I'm cool with the old-fashioned way. Since Carlos and I have a history, so he was my best choice. He and I have a bond we made years ago. I was pregnant with his child during my junior year of college. While hanging out with my lesbian friends, some guys kept trying to get us to talk to them. One of my friends flicked them off, and we got into a shoving match. I left before my friends. One of the guys followed me out and tried to rape me. I fought back, but he overpowered me. I miscarried. I didn't want to be around men for a long time. Carlos gave me my space but never let me forget how he felt about me. He's been on the fringes of my life ever since then. Sophie has no clue about that part of my past, but she likes Carlos, so she put him through her sperm donor test. He met her requirements, including being an intelligent, successful, healthy, and handsome man of color. Carlos has a Latina mother and a black father. Sophie is mixed also, which gives Carlos bonus points.

It didn't take long for me to get pregnant. We have a two-year-old son named Christian. Sophie was there both times, making love to me with Carlos. I had never thought about a polyamorous relationship until then. I enjoyed it, and I honestly love both of them. The sex was magical. Sophie engaged with Carlos more than I thought she would. I haven't cleared up how I truly feel about that.

We had an agreement that Sophie now wants to change. She planned to get pregnant after Christian turned two, provided we could afford it. Sophie says she is ready, but our finances are not.

"Okay, I will just have to do it as you did."

"Sophie, let's just wait a little longer."

"Christian needs a playmate. "

"I thought you were against the idea of penetration with a guy."

"I don't hate it. I've thought about being with a man many times."

"Since when?" I asked.

"Since we were with Carlos?"

"Really."

"I was apprehensive because guys can be rough, but Carlos was gentle with you."

"Oh, so you took notes."

"Not really, I observed how you opened up to him, and he made sure you were satisfied."

"We have history, Sophie. He knows my body."

"Are you saying he will not do the same with me?"

"That is not what I'm saying."

"Then, what?"

She didn't wait for my response. "You are not cool with me having sex with Carlos," I said nothing.

"Tell me the truth, Zoe."

"You're right I don't," I said emphatically.

"Why?"

"Because I don't, and it's non-negotiable," I said walking out of the room. I could feel Sophie's eyes stabbing me in the back. The conversation was far from over.

Get Up Stand Up

F AYEMI.

I'm an aggressive bisexual-born Muslim. Males respond to my aggressiveness favorably, but women do not so much. Most women are primarily curious or non-accepting lesbians. They are fun to engage with but limited in the potential for commitment. I desire someone that smells like strength. Maybe I'm a product of my upbringing. The men and women of our faith are very strong-willed and disciplined. I'm afraid I have to disagree with all of the tenets of the faith, but those two things are a requirement of my potential mate. I have hopes for a woman like that, but a man can also take the front seat in my life.

Curious or non-accepting lesbians seem to have their radar set on me. I've had fun with it, but now it

has gotten old. We hang out. They like me. Before we have sex, I tell them I'm bisexual. They poke around, thinking they can change me. My preference for women is extreme. My gay friends think I'm a closeted lesbian. The straight ones think

I'm buying time until I find the right man. Neither group believes bisexuality is a legitimate orientation. I gave up trying to dispute this a long time ago. No matter what they say, I know what is natural for me.

I'm the oldest of three children. My identical twin, Adeeb, is older by minutes. It's true what they say about twins being able to feel things about each other. When Adeeb broke his leg. I felt pain in mine.

When I get sick, he gets sick. Even when I started my period, he felt cramping. We share many things, but he is more passive than I am. On our tenth birthday, I told him I liked girls.

"So what do I like, boys."

"I like boys too," I said, thinking I one-upped him.

"So. I like girls." He said trying to one-up me.

"Stop lying," I said.

"I'm not lying. But I've known for a long time you liked girls."

"Adeeb! You read my journal." I said, punching him on the arm.

"Ouch! Stop hitting me, Faye. I know you like I know me. I'm your twin."

"Why didn't you say anything?" Faye shouted attempting to punch Adeeb. He blocked it.

"I don't know." He said. "I guess because it's weird."

"I'm not weird," I said, punching at him again.

"Stop it, Faye," He said grabbing her by the shoulders. She wriggles away. Adeeb gets very solemn.

"It's not normal. We are not normal, he said. And what if Dad finds out?"

"He won't," I said.

All the bantering and joking were replaced by the reality that who we were was not what society calls normal. We stood there looking at each other for a moment. The despair in Adeeb's eyes deepened. Dad finding out about him would be more brutal than for me. Adeeb would be kicked into the streets. And I would be forced to marry some man that would invariably be horrible to me. The worst part is Adeeb's name would not be allowed to be spoken again. He would be dead to us. I wanted to assure him more but I knew he was right. I could only promise him. "I'll never tell your secret."

Even though I wouldn't ever out my brother, the taboo of bisexuality didn't cause me any fear for real. Knowing I wasn't alone was a relief. Sure, I wrestled with the idea of being weird, different, and alone. For weeks my brother was all I could think about. The negativity, violence, and abuse I heard made me afraid to look at girls. Being bisexual for the ignorant meant being promiscuous, and I wasn't even having sex. It is called simply being Gay and it's not welcomed into our house or faith. Our parents were open-minded about many worldly ideologies, but not in our home.

My connection with Adeeb took on a whole new meaning shrouded in secrecy. We only communicated about our attractions or teenage crushes when we were not in the house. We discovered at least one thing that

101

didn't translate and the twin sameness, we had the opposite taste in girls and boys. It became a competition to see whose crush was the sexiest. The sense of competition was not new to us. That began in the womb. I believe I saw the exit vagina light first.

I think it went something like this, "Hold up, this could be a false alarm. Let me go check it out."

It's all in fun though. Our parents encouraged us to strive for excellence. Our competitive edge is only one pushing the other to achieve it.

We kept each other secret for a long time. A week before high school graduation, we were eating breakfast before going to the Mosque. My father was reticent. Adeeb was late to the table as usual.

"Sorry," Adeeb said rushing in half dressed. He pulled out his chair.

"Don't sit," Father said as he pushed away from the table."Come with me."

Something in my father's tone created a silence I recognized. We all recognized it as we looked at one another. Something serious was about to go down. The last time Father had that tone, my Uncle Kenyatta was the recipient. He's my mother's younger brother and leader of the Free Speech Nation. A group of Muslims pushing for reform of the faith's rules on marriage, same-sex relationships, and a woman's right to choose. Uncle Kenyatta challenged my father's views.

"You are blind to the hypocrisy in all religions." He said.

My father ignored him. Uncle Kenyatta took this as an opening for him to continue his dissertation.

"You are a born-again Christian who fought in a war for a country that sees you as a second-class citizen. Now you are a Muslim as if that is any better."

Uncle Kenyatta struck a nerve, Father looked at him directly. My uncle should have stopped there. But he kept going.

"You are trying to escape the realities of the hypocrisy of one faith and replaced it with one equally hypocritical."

Father stood up and pointed to the door. Uncle Kenyatta kept talking. Without saying a word, Father walked over to him, grabbed him by his collar, and tossed him out of our house. That was three years ago.

Uncle Kenyatta has not been back to our home.

This morning felt eerily like that day. Father and Adeeb disappeared. Father returned without Adeeb as were finishing breakfast. No one dared question Father. We went to the Mosque without Adeeb. As soon as I got home I burst into Adeeb's room.

"What happened?"

"Fayemi, what happened to knock?"

"Shut up. What happened with Father?"

"Brother Kwame told him he saw pictures of me and some other boys on Facebook."

"What were you doing?"

"Nothing."

"So what's the big deal?"

"We were standing in front of the Chocolate Factory."

"The Chocolate Factory! Are you crazy? That's the gayest bar in the city."

"Did you tell him it was just a picture and… ?"

"He didn't ask for an explanation. He said if I don't submit to understanding that associating with people and places like that can put me under the devil's control and atone for my mistake, don't be here when he gets back".

"And you are still here."

"Fayemi, I'm not willing to blow my future over this."

"Maybe I should tell him about me."

"Great, and then we both lose out."

"Lose out on what? If we tell him he has two queer children, maybe we can change his mind about the whole thing."

"Stop saying, queer. I don't like that word."

"Stop being a wuss," I said.

"Get out of my room, Faye."

"I'm sorry. It's just not fair, that's all."

"Look, he said, we are about to go to college in a few months."

"Exactly, we are almost on our own. Let's go tell him now." I stood up to go out the door. Adeeb blocked me.

"No, we are not. We will be freshmen without jobs.

Father will cut us off, and then what."

"Adeeb, we can manage. Stop being a wu...."

"Do you, Faye. I'm riding this out."

I hated to admit it, but Adeeb was right. We needed to buy some time considering the challenges of a freshman in college. If I had to get another job on top of school, I would have been back home before the midterms. College life is a different world than high school. The professors don't care about your workload. You are expected to be an adult and know how to manage time. Fortunately for us, our parents taught us time management. I wish someone had prepared me for my roommate Teresa.

It's passé but true in my case. My first encounter with sex was with my roommate. Nothing exciting; Teresa was not my type. Adeeb thought she was hot. Teresa has thin lips that barely smile and are naturally turned down into a pout. Her skin is pale with yellow undertones, and her hair is red, so her eyebrows blend into her skin. As you can guess, she is not African American or a Catholic.

Around the third week of classes, my roomy

started a masturbation ritual. She went to bed before me and would begin as soon as I settled in. I assumed she was dreaming but who masturbates for 20 minutes in a dream? The following day she would pretend as if nothing had happened. This went on for weeks. I pretended not to notice for as long as I could, but her sounds and the apparent pleasure she was getting kept pulling me in. I would listen until she climaxed. I would then lie in exhaustion as if it had been me.

As is customary of the faith, my parents chose someone for me to marry. Kareem is a lieutenant in the faith and five years older than me. Our families know each other very well, so it was no surprise. I accepted the idea because it is our way, but I prayed Allah would intervene. I wanted to honor the faith and the freedom to marry whomever I chose. Kareem is a great guy. He's well-respected, a college graduate owns a couple of convenience stores, and is handsome in a brotherly way. He was not as locked into the rules of the faith as the elders thought. He and I messed around a couple of times. He wanted to go all the way. I wasn't ready for that, especially not with him.

I was relieved when he called it off. But I was angry about how he did it. I was walking through the Quad to my dorm when he text me. We need to talk. I immediately called him back thinking something was wrong. My heart was racing.

"I don't want to marry you." He said.

"Umm.. hello."

"I've found someone else, and we've been seeing each other for a while."

"What you've been cheating on me?"

"I'm so sorry, Faye."

"You are sorry. A sorry-ass excuse for a man." I said.

"Fayemi, you can't tell me you didn't see this coming."

I wanted to lie and say no. My pride was hurt but I let him off the hook. I was still upset that he had been cheating on me, but I couldn't deny that I was happy. I couldn't wait to tell my family.

When I hung up the phone, all I could say was, "Alhamdulillah, thanks, and praise to Allah." Then I jumped up and down like I had scored a touchdown until I noticed a crowd of people in the hallway of my dorm. The closer I got I could see they were at my door.

"What's going on?"

Some girl whispered, "Sounds like your roomie has company."

I could hear the familiar moans from the hall, but much louder and accompanied by, "Yes, yes, harder, harder…."

"Move," I said.

I pushed everyone aside and flung open the door.

"What the hell?"

Teresa was lying on the bed with some girl's head between her legs.

"I thought you were out for the night."

"Do I need to leave until you finish, or can I go to bed in my room?"

"It's our room. You can stay if you want." The girl pulled the covers over her head.

"I'll come back later."

I backed out of the room, taking the waiting crowd

with me. Teresa was awake and ready to talk when I returned. "You know, I'm not out."

"I don't care."

"Please keep this on the down low."

"Nobody has to know," I said in my best R. KELLY.

"I'm serious. Faye"

"Fayemi," I corrected her. Only family and close friends call me Faye. " What you do is your business?"

"Faye, I mean Fayemi. That name is too damn long."

I shot her an evil look.

"No disrespect, damn! I'm just saying, I'm cool but Shorty is paranoid. "

"Okay, what does that have to do with me? I don't know her?"

"Shawn."

"GSA Shawn?"

Teresa nodded yes.

"She's the president of the gayest organization on campus and she's in the closet," I said in disbelief.

"That's not it, she has a girlfriend," Teresa

remarked.

"Oh snap. That's wrong."

"So, we kick it sometimes. I'm not the one with the girlfriend. That's on her."

"It's whatever. What would I say, hey Shawn's girlfriend? I saw a naked girl eating out my roommate. By the way, I think it was Shawn. I could blackmail her into supporting bisexuals more in that lame organization."

"Stop playing Fayemi."

"Do you get it? I don't care. Do what you do. Just do it somewhere else."

"This is my room too. I can have anyone in it whenever I want."

"Not if I tell the RA"

"I dare you."

"You don't want to try me, Teresa."

"Is that a threat?"

"A promise."

"Ooh Muslim girl got some spunk. I like that in you." Teresa pats me on the ass.

"Stop playing," I shouted.

"Seriously, I will tell you if I plan to have someone in the room. Shawn won't be coming back. She and her girl are having problems but haven't called it quits yet."

"Why get in the middle of that drama?"

"I'm having fun. I'm not ready for anything more than getting some head here and there. I think we like each other, but it's strictly sexual. And I'm good with that."

We resumed our daily schedule. Teresa had begun amping up masturbation to the point where I could hear her fingers sliding in and out with a sloshing sound. She was popping them in and out. It sounded like she was sucking her thumb too. Something came over me, and my curiosity took over.

After a few nights of her doing that, I crawled into bed with her. It lasted 15 minutes. It was okay, but I had nothing to compare it to. I let her eat me, but I was not about to return the favor. At the time, it seemed unsanitary, considering Teresa's active sex life. We attempted to do it again but realized we were better as roomy friends. However, the sex did make us a little closer. When I had challenges, I could talk to her. Teresa helped me decide to join the GSA after attending a protest against the athletic department for firing the basketball coach because she was gay.

"Why should I join? They say they exist to provide a forum for LGBT students to play a role in the politics of the campus and protection from sexual orientation, but they discriminate against the bisexuals."

"There are not many bisexuals on campus."

"How do you know?" I growled.

"I don't, but where are they to prove me wrong?"

"That's a stupid question. They have no support."

"Exactly; if they won't stand up for themselves, nothing changes."

"We need a forum. I'm sure we can start an organization."

"What we? Organizing may be easy, but whom will you organize? They don't come out. "

"They would if they had support."

"How do you expect change to happen?"

"Ideally, everyone does it on their own. But most often, it happens when all the old people leave or die, and the young take over with new ideas."

"Why wait? Bring the new ideas."

I thought it over for a few days. In the meantime, I encountered other bisexuals on campus who felt like I felt but were not ready to take a step. After thinking about it more, I agreed with Teresa. Change happens when someone decides they want to do something. I certainly couldn't wait for anyone on campus to do it, or it may never happen. At the next open enrollment meeting, I joined. Shawn's face was the first one I saw when I walked in. Allah, please take me the way. Shawn was stunning with long dark hair, caramel skin, thick lips, and deep b, brown eyes. Even though there were no fireworks, the ground did move under me.

Before long, I was a card-carrying bisexual identifying as a lesbian in the gay community. The card is theoretical, but my point is that I joined a movement that had a label for every possible orientation. Bisexuals were the least respected but made up the majority. They just kept quiet about it and blended in.

When Adeeb found out, he tried to persuade me to quit. "Group affiliations before you have secured your future is dangerous," he said. "There you go putting the cart before the horse."

"What are you saying? When you lay down with Mayor Davis, you sleep with one of the biggest groups."

"Yes, but he is leverage."

"Explain," I said.

"Being in the forefront of any group is risky business. So you find an ally within a group that may be able to help you move into a position to make bigger changes. Feel things out first. Figure out how it will benefit you. Planning and preparation come with time and patience."

"Who died and anointed you, Buddha?"

"Buddha? Really? Don't be such a smart ass."

"I'm serious. It's dangerous being us, but we can change things if we are strategic about it."

"When did you get so wise?"

"I was born this way. And so were you."

Adeeb was right again. He was on a mission that placed him in a position to pursue his interest. We shared a dream to make it to the Supreme Court. His words reminded me of that dream.

Inside the GSA, I observed the mockery of bisexuality. Persons who identified as bisexual were pressured into choosing one gender over the other. They were given tasks no one else wanted. None held a decision-making position. I attributed it to the organization that is new to the campus. I thought about what Adeeb had said. I needed to be more strategic.

Teresa noticed Shawn and me hanging out together a lot. If we were not doing something for the GSA, we were helping with voter registration and other community-related issues. Out of the blue, she says, "Did you know Shawn and her girl were no longer together."

"She told me," I remarked.

"You know, I wouldn't be mad if you and she started seeing each other."

"We see each other every day," I said mockingly.

"You know what I mean. If you decided to hook up

with her, I would be perfectly cool with that."

I wasn't sure how to respond. Shawn told me she and Teresa were done after we laughed about the infamous night. Teresa confirmed they never hooked up again. I should have paid more attention to Teresa's body language and less to her words. Instead, I spilled my guts.

"Thanks, Tee. I appreciate that. I was concerned you may still have feelings for her."

"I said I liked her. I said nothing about feelings."

"Cool. I'm relieved. Shawn and I slept together a week ago."

"Does she know you are bisexual?"

"Yes, why?"

"She told me she would never be with a bisexual because they are flighty, greedy, and indecisive."

"All of that has changed. I'm working on her overall opinion of bisexuals." Teresa's demeanor changed. She abruptly ended the conversation. This moment with her would come back to haunt me.

By the end of the semester, the GSA appeared to be

in the same shape as when I first joined. The more I ignored things, the more I watched the numbers dwindle. I saw the disillusionment and hopelessness in the eyes of those we were supposed to be helping. I tried addressing it head-on with Shawn.

"How can the GSA fight for acceptance while promoting separatism from within? Faye, bisexuality is a phase, not a designation. Anyone who identifies with it is confused. Confused people can't lead."

"Are you kidding me?"

Had she forgotten whom she was talking to? I let her speak and pretended to be calm when she was done. I had to talk to my brother first. He advised me to rally my supporters and run against her when the time came for elections. I did, and I won. Shawn and I broke up. The organization now has rules of conduct and methods for tolerance of differences that do not insult or disrespect anyone. Of course, it is an uphill battle. One of my advisors invited me to join another group that meets periodically. It's a bunch of older bisexual women who live out loud. I'll check it out, I guess. I'm so over people talking about a good game.

This better not be that.

On the home front, my parents are getting over themselves and having two, I mean three, children in unconventional love relationships. Our youngest sister has decided she wants to be a nun.

JUSTICE UNPLUGGED

My heart started racing when I read her message."I heard this song, and it made me think of you. I miss the fun we used to have."

Daniel walked in with my cup of coffee.

"Do you want my hand to fall off?" he asked.

In my best Billie H,oliday I sang. "I must have that man."

"Do you need anything else, baby?" Daniel said.

"No, lover, I'm good."

Her message played in my mind as I absorbed Daniel. The perfect cup of coffee. I had to pray. Lord, someone lay hands on me."The universe delivers me only what I can handle. I am looking for the feeling of love I discovered with her. When I sleep, I can feel it. I can't see her face anymore, but it feels like the love I found with her. I feel it when I open my eyes and see him."

Tamia sings one of my favorites, Me. The radiothat has been on all day finally catches my attention.

"Okay," I said.

"Did you call me?" Daniel yelled from the other room.

"No, lover, but since you are here, how about we turn on some Maxwell and do it til the cops come knocking."

In the heterosexual community, it's easier to mask female same-sex attraction These women are easily identifiable and will be almost fanatical about being strictly dickly. A large majority of heterosexual-identified women who are bisexual blame their girl's night sexcapades on alcohol. Out of fear of never finding companionship, in any community, she may blend into one over the other. Being on the leading edge of existence, she knows how to adapt convincingly and can flow in and out of both if necessary. Her sexuality in a mixed environment will be non-topical, and she will actively avoid discussing it. Successfully blending helps her achieve mastery in the art of the Power of Influence.

The Art In
POWER of
INFLUENCE

A STREAMING VIBRATION FELT WHEN
YOU CAN LOOK AT ANY SITUATION
FOR THE POSITIVITY IT INSPIRES
ESPECIALLY WHEN WHAT YOU ARE
LOOKING AT APPEARS TO BE
IMPOSSIBLE
To break barriers, and bridge social
divides

The African American bisexual woman has come to teach through the clarity of her example what loving without conditions looks like. She will not and cannot be socialized in conformity. This is the same for many born with situations they cannot change even if they want to. Sexual orientation is decided before it is manifested.

Too Good To Be True

E NID.

Dear God…

It's me, Gayle. I could get into the whole story of my childhood, a failed marriage, and all that jazz, but it pales compared to what I'm living. Besides, you know all about me. I have stage five cancer. I don't know how to feel about it. My partner is trying to walk with her head high, but she is scared. We've been together for 15 years, twenty if you count the five spent with me delivering her mail. Enid is a nurturer who no longer has an outlet in me. I'm leaving this place. She's scared. She'll be here without me. She refuses to talk about it. I want her to be happy, but it doesn't seem very easy for

me to say. Instead of wasting time trying, I crack jokes.
She laughs sometimes but not too often. I want to see her
eyes light up again like they used to.

"Come closer to me, Enid. I need to talk to you."

"I'm right here, Gayle."

" Can you feel me?" Enid said.

"There you are. This feels like the first night we met. Do you remember us spooning?"

"I remember," Gayle said.

"I did you first."

"For about two minutes, then you said, do me."

"And you held me for the rest of the night."

"What will you do when I croak?" "Don't say it like that"Enid said. "Why not? It sounds funny."

"It is not funny."

"I'm the one dealing with this shit. If I say it's funny, it's funny."

Gayle says she's at peace with her disease. She's convinced it's her punishment for being gay. Her self-imposed atonement convinced her that the church should get all her resources in tithes and inheritance. Last year we faced bankruptcy as a result of her obsession. Her history with the church is almost insane. First of all, Gayle was married to a man, a deacon. He was physically and emotionally abusive. The church encouraged her to stay and work it out. After almost dying from his beating her, she took their children and ran as far away from him as possible. The church still tried to get them back together. That's crazy to me, but she is faithful with her tithes. We recovered from the financial setback, but her giving is still excessive. Gayle thinks I was raised in a non-denominational family, so I can't understand how it works. Sure, my parents never forced religion, but tithing is not my biggest issue with organized religion. The hypocrisy is what gets me. I joined Salvation's Rock with her. She had been a member for over a year but never officially joined. I fell in love with the gay-friendly atmosphere and the music. It was the only church in the city where I felt rise when I heard the choir. Sometimes I would leave after praise and worship. Quite frankly, it was all I needed to hear. The sermons were to fire and brimstone for my taste. Everything was going great until the Sunday after Prop 8 was overturned. The preacher berated California's ruling as an abomination. He said, "God loves us all but being gay is like any other illness. It must be treated with medication, or it rots the body."

I was livid. Gayle didn't flinch. "Gayle, this is bullshit."

"Enid, we are in a church."

"A church that condemns you and me and the other gay people I know are sitting here listening to this crap after putting money in the collection plate."

"Keep your voice down. Being gay is a choice to sin against God. I made a choice, so I suffered. We all do."

"Show me the scripture that supports that."

"Enid, let it go."

"I will not let it go. Our tithing almost single-handedly keeps these damn doors open. And you are okay with this?" I said. "Enid, let it go."

"Are you blind?" Gayle refused to answer.

"This seems like a pattern," I said. "You let your ex walk all over you, and now this church."

As soon as the words left my mouth, life for me was about to take a severe turn. Gayle kicked me out of our bedroom. I could have protested, but I refused to back down this time. Things needed to change.

Her obsession with her illness being punishment was tearing us apart.

Gayle's doctors prepared us for the changes she would undergo as the disease progressed.

"Cancer eats away your dignity, long before it takes your body," they said.

"She has the most aggressive form. It moves throughout the body very rapidly. The pain will worsen as it spreads. The Percocet will help but may be ineffective as the disease progresses."

"Great, I will go from bad to worse. Thanks for the wonderful report, as if just dying wasn't enough." Gayle said.

"What about other medication?" I asked.

"There is morphine," said the doctor. "I'll be dead by then." She said. "Gayle, please."

Her indifference was maddening. I wanted to

scream out, what about me? Is this all you got for me? Five damn doctors and no one can give me my Gayle back. What was the point in knowing how bad it would get when there was nothing anyone could do about it? The nurse pulled me aside. "Here is the number to a cancer support group. It's a safe place to say things like I wish it were over and not be judged as insensitive."

"How did you know?" I asked relieved someone was able to articulate what I've thinking but was too ashamed to share it.

"My sister had cancer. The entire family had a hard time adjusting. She saw us struggling and wanted to do something to help us while we waited for the inevitable. With the help of her husband Steve, she created a safe place for the family of cancer patients to speak to and hear from cancer"' She searched for something to write on. "Steve is still the facilitator of the group. They meet twice a week focusing on ways to cope because the closer it gets to that time the more reality intensifies."

I cried myself to sleep that night and the night after

that and after that. I couldn't imagine being without her. I wanted to die with her.

I learned from the first few meetings that Steve's wife died six months after she started the group. He kept it going in honor of her memory. On the surface, the group addresses cancer issues. However, it's so much more. It helps people own their power over their circumstances. When I decided to share openly and honestly I could not shut up. "I'm afraid to be alone. And I'm mad at her for leaving me."

Once I heard myself say it aloud, I felt a massive weight off my chest. I thought it was awesome that no one tried to silence my sobs because I was used to people telling me not to cry. I needed to call. Without judgment, the group offered suggestions on how to cope. One person shared how the use of marijuana was helping her mother stay calm and play nice. That made me laugh. The next day I contacted her doctors to get a marijuana prescription. The prices sure have increased. The next time I contacted a friend of a friend of a friend and got some excellent inexpensive, untaxed stuff. Gayle and I smoked together. Sex is on the table again.

She usually falls asleep before anything jumps off, but things look up. I am back in the bedroom.

The other day she fell out of bed trying to get up to go to the bathroom. I rushed over to help, but she brushed me off.

"Honey, you know it's not a good idea for you to do that by yourself."

"I'm a grown-ass woman."

"Yes, but you are not strong enough right now for some things."

She tried again unsuccessfully, ultimately allowing me the opportunity to help.

"I'm going to look into getting a nurse to come in for a few hours daily," I said.

"I don't need no damn nurse?" "What if I wasn't here and you fell." "I would get up eventually."

"Gayle, it's not a good idea for you to be alone when I'm not here."

"Listen, Enid; I don't need you. I don't need a nurse. I don't need anybody. You can get out right now." She said.

"I'm a grown-ass woman too, and I'm not going anywhere. So get over yourself." I said.

I moved into the guest room temporarily again.

It was best because her pain and agitation throughout the night startled me. I couldn't rest well, which was another reason I needed some help. Her insurance company approved her as a nurse for four hours a day. Just enough time for me to have some breathing room and know she is safe.

Gayle's condition is not getting better; I know that. I'm so grateful for the support of Steve and the group. Steve has been such a strong ally. I lean on him often, and he is there for me whenever I call. I've never thought about being with a man intimately, even though I've loved them all my life.

Dear God…

It's me, Gayle. I'm so over this pain. I know I'm acting crazy sometimes. All of the pain medicine and the weed helps, but I realize I'm not accepting my reality. I'm angry. I'm dying. It's not fair to Enid, but what can I do? I'm so mad and frustrated with cancer. I feel like I've been punched, cheated, and blindsided by something I don't deserve. I knew what was going on with my husband. It took me a while, but I did leave. When I did, I declared my freedom and never looked back or at anyone for anything. Look at me now. Cancer is taking me down. I cannot do things for myself, and I will die. I never thought it would go down like this. I want to do better by Enid. I have to. She gave me a book by Wayne Dyer the other day called Change Your Thoughts Change Your Life. I said I wasn't going to read it; I'm glad I changed my mind. Maybe it's the weed messing with my head.

I know people who go through years in a sexless relationship by choice. Others have it forced upon them. Gayle and I used to have sex all the time. When she injured her back, we worked around it. I put in all the work for one of the best years of my life. Cancer is forcing us to be abstinent, and I still have desires.

Something else is happening. Gayle changed her

will to make me the executor. I had no idea she was doing it until the signing. She is worth well over a million dollars and has investments in an organization called Club Beijui. Her family and the church are up in arms. They think I made her change her will to leave everything to me. It almost came to blows between her daughter and me. I called Steve and got the hell out of there.

"It's happening. It's happening."

"What?" Steve asked.

"The will...everybody wants to argue over the damn money. I didn't ask for it. I don't want it. I want her. I can't do this. I want to die with her."

"Enid! Look at me. You will survive."

"No, I won't."

"Yes, you will."

"I don't want to."

"I need you too."

No more words were said. Steve wrapped me in his arms. I don't know how long he held me. The vibration of my phone broke the embrace.

"Enid, you need to come home right away."

Dear God...

It's me, Gayle. The days are getting longer. I'm so tired.

I think Enid is ready. I think I am too.

When I got home, Gayle was gasping for air. The nurse was holding her hand. I motioned for the nurse to let me take over. Gayle looks so frail now. I don't want her to suffer any longer. I know it's only a matter of time. I can't leave her alone. The group meets at my home now. They all know. When she can find the energy, Gayle sits in as another voice of the disease. Tonight she could barely complete a sentence. After the meeting, I walked Steve to the car. Tears erupted, and I couldn't stop. He held me as he did before.

"Call me if you need me to come back." He said.

This time I didn't wait for him to hold me. Resting my head on his chest, I sobbed."This is it."

"I'm only a phone call away."

I held on to Steve for dear life. Time moved slowly.

All the years with Gayle rushed through me. The safety of Steve's arms was my eternity.

Gayle was waiting up for me. Seeing her sitting up gave me a twinge of possibility. She hadn't sat up in weeks without someone helping her.

"Look at you."

"Is there something you want to tell me?" she asked. I kissed her face and brushed the threads of hair from her face. "I love you," I whispered, barely able to hide how difficult seeing her had become. She placed her hand on my cheek. I felt the woman I had fallen in love with. I put my head over her heart.

She stroked my head. Her breathing was so shallow. I knew it was done. I heard her take her last breaths that night, and she went to sleep.

Weeks later, while cleaning Gayle's room, her journal fell from under the pillow. I'm not ready to do much more than that. I turned to her last entry.

My Dearest Enid…

It's me, Gayle. They said our relationship was too good

to be true. I felt that way, too, at first. But after all of the challenges, we are still here. That first meeting was pure love. It inspired all of the beautiful days after. We didn't even have to try. We fought for it. The stars lined up just for us. I remember the spark of hope in you. I put so much on you, and with this disease, your light dimmed. Over the past few weeks, I have seen the sparkle is back —that fire. I'm so happy to see it. It's okay. Steve has good energy. Go on. Be happy. I'll be around—no need to ever wonder. When the stars align, it's too good not to be true.

Love always,

Gayle

Turnt

K HALEESI.
My spirit can't be contained. Family, friends, and lovers all know this about me. At one time, I thought it was selfish to be so free and happy when so many around me were not. Then I came to my senses. I earned every bit of my happiness. I've done

more damage trying to be something I wasn't than being myself.

I've reconnected with an old lover after ten years. It's frisky, spontaneous, dynamic, intellectually stimulating, easy, exciting, sensual, and respectful. If I could only get him to be okay with my girlfriend, Tatiana, my world would be complete. I was fourteen, naive, and bumped when I met Trey at a block party. He was eighteen and very mature.

WHO IS BOO JACK

The summer of 2012 was the hottest summer ever. My mom and I moved from country living to the big city. It was a culture shock but the community was very welcoming. We arrived just in time for the annual block party. Everyone participated in some way. Mr. Jones from down the block provided the electricity for the DJ. Crazy Joe handled the kids' games, and the pool runs. The kids splashed out faster than he could put it in. Momma Sookie organized the food, and everybody brought alcohol.

Ms. Carrie Anne lived across the street from us.

Her daughter Pam took me under her wing. At first, the other girls stared me up and down but never said anything to me. Then they started calling me a "high yellow girl with good hair." Ms. Carrie Anne saw them picking on me one day; Pam invited me to sit on her stoop the next day. No one messed with me after that. Pam's family ran the block. Even if the other girls didn't like me, they still had to back off.

I was moving too slowly to the center of the block because Pam was beckoning me like she was about to pee. Suddenly there was this loud drum roll, and the crowd went crazy. The closer we got we heard what sounded like a drill sergeant giving instructions. I thought it was the JROTC from our school. When we turned the corner, someone shouted, "Drop the Beat"The crowd parted, and eleven brothers were standing in line formation wearing hoodies with no sleeves, black khakis, and Timberlands.

"Brothers, are you ready."

"We stay ready."

"Brothers, are you ready."

"To rock steady."

The guy in the middle stepped forward and started stumping out a beat. The two on his left and right stepped up and joined until everyone was on the same line again, and everybody was rocking. They stumped so hard that Mrs. Smith's, the neighborhood gossip, wig tilted to the side. It almost looked like it did the time she drank a whole jar of corn liquor. Mr. Smith was drunk and needed help going into his house. They both fell. Her wig went to the left, and she went to the right. Everybody started laughing. Mrs. Smith just grabbed her wig and slapped it on her head. It was backward, but she didn't care. She cussed Mr. Smith out.

There were so many people on the block. I had never seen so many people in one place except at a funeral. The whole scene was intoxicating. I couldn't keep my eyes off the guy in the middle. He caught me staring at him, and then he wouldn't stop looking at me. As soon as the show was over, he ran in my direction. Venus Price, the neighborhood gold digger, cut him off.

"Wassup, Boo Jack? Where are you going?" He proceeded to walk in her direction."Got to get more buns for the hot dogs. Don't leave before I get back."

"Okay, but why don't I just go with you?" She said as Boo Jack walked past her.

"I'm not talking to you, Venus."He said as he stopped directly in front of me. I didn't know what to do or say. Venus was staring me up and down. Boo Jack took my hand.

"Don't worry about her."

"Is she your girlfriend?" I whispered.

"No. That's just my Baby Mama." He laughed, "She's cool as a fan, but sometimes she starts tripping."

"Should I be worried?"

Trey turned around to see Venus eyeballing me.

"She'll be right," returning his gaze. "But I won't if you leave before I get back."

Pam came out of nowhere. "Keep it moving, Tre. This one's jail bait."

"Pam, I'm just saying hi."

Trey escapes her attempt to mush him. "Will you be

here when I get back, baby?" "Why?" Pam retorted.

Trey shot Pam an evil look. "I'm not talking to you." I wasn't sure if I should speak or let them both keep talking as if I was not standing there. I decided to jump in.

"I guess so," I said.

"What's your name?" Trey said.

"Khaleesi." "Boo Jackson."

Pam stepped in between us. She was a few inches taller than him. Looking slightly down at him, she said.

"Tee, go before I tell Mama."

"Tell Mama I said hi to…."

"You can't even say her name."

"It's Khaleesi, but my friends call me Lee." "Okay, Lee." He said, moving away from Pam. "Stay here and ignore my sister. She's a hater."

Pam reached for him. He side-stepped her attempt and disappeared into the crowd.

"What's up with that, Pam?"

"Girl, that's my brother, and he is a man."

"Your brother? Why did he say his name was Boo

something. "

"His name is Trey. Boo, Jackson is his line name. Boo Jack for short."

"He is fine."

"He is too old for your young ass," Pam said.

"I think he's sexy."

"He's in college, and you are in high school."

"What did you mean when you said line name?" I asked.

"You are too young. Trey pledged with a fraternity. Being online means being in the process of pledging or something like that. Anyway, they gave him the nickname Boo Jackson."

"Oh, I heard that, but I didn't know what it meant." I tried to sound like I was telling the truth. Pam wasn't buying it.

"Sure you have. So you know what a step show is too?"

"I'm not an idiot," I said.

Pam was beginning to get on my nerves.

"I'll let that go, young, but my brother, stay away

from him. He has too much going on."

"What's the problem? I'm not that much younger than him."

"Yeah, but his life is filled with grownup shit." She said.

My confused face encouraged her to continue even though I could sense she wanted to get back on the block.

"Don't get me wrong. Trey is a good dude. He has many responsibilities."

"Like what?"

"Like kids."

"And? So what, he has a kid."

"You didn't hear me. He has kids, plural."

"Venus, is his baby Mama, right?"

"She is one of them. He has two babies, Mama's, and three kids. Venus has one, and the other girl, I forget her name, has one and a possible. The paternity test hasn't come back yet."

"So there is only one for real."

Pam continued, "Maybe, but Trey does not think

before he gets with them, girls. He's brilliant. But all the brains in the world can't keep his dick covered."

Pam kept talking, but I didn't hear her. We finally walked around the block, taking in all of the excitement. My mind was swirling with thoughts. Without knowing all of that about Trey, my first feelings felt good. Pam's words had tainted them, but how could I have felt such a strong pull toward him if he was all wrong form? When our eyes met, it was like nothing else had ever existed outside of that moment. I didn't want to care about what Pam said. I didn't want to think about it. I liked how he looked at me. It felt good to be looked at like that. I had been very insecure with my body. I was coming out of my chunky phase. I didn't find myself attractive, nor could I imagine a college guy as fine as Trey ever wanting to talk to me.

I hung around until Trey returned, but between

Pam's cock blocking and Venus gritting on me, Trey and I did not get a chance to talk that day. There was no room for me.

TWO YEARS LATER

Bass booty music is playing. Coolers are filled with a purple passion—kegs of beer line the back fence. Moonshine is chilling with Uncle Pete in the garage, and the DJ is rocking the bells. The block party is now a Street Festival with two stages, one for the adults and the other for the kids. One block has now turned into four. It was hotter than hell, and I wanted to rock something cool and sexy.

I grabbed my daisy dukes and my tube top. My titties were still itty bitties, so I stuffed socks under them to make them look plump. I didn't make it out the door before one fell out. I pulled out the other one and tossed them in the corner. The momentum of the music was calling me. It signaled the beginning of the step show. "Maybe he will be here this year." I kept thinking.

Pam was yelling for me to hurry up.

"Come on, Lee. We need to get a good spot."

"I'm coming," I said, trying to keep up.

"The steppers are about to set it off, and all

fraternities are representing this year."

He could be here this year. I moved as fast as I could. As I looked up the street, the crowd gathered near the main stage. It was packed to the brim with spectators. The fraternities were grouped in sections before the stage with their respective sister sororities. I searched the faces until I saw him. At first, I couldn't

DownLow July 21 Thirsty

see his face because his back was turned toward me, and one of the sororities was doing something to his hoodie. His back still faced me when she moved, but I knew it was him. I would know their legs and that tight ass anywhere.

"You see, Trey," Pam asked.

"Hell yeah, I see him. Oh my God. Your brother is still fine as hell."

"Oh lord. There you go."

"You know he is."

"Yeah, I do."

"No cock blocking this year, Pam."

"Who me?"

"Yes, you."

The show was the fire. Trey bolted over to me after, but Venus did not stop him this time. He and I dipped to his mom's house while everybody else was at the festival. I lost my virginity that day. It was everything I imagined and then some. The plastic on his Mama's couch was sticking to my ass. Trey pinned my legs around my ears.

"Let me feel all of you," I said.

"Baby, this is all I got."

"No, stupid, take off the condom."

"Oh, you have bumped your head, girl?" "I can't get pregnant."

"Doesn't matter."

"I mean, I can but not now. I'm not ovulating."

"Lee, chill and roll over."

"What?"

"Shut up and roll over."

"Okay."

Looking back on that day, I hear how stupid I sounded. Trey was gentle and patient with me. He twisted my virgin body inside and out, giving me space to explore what I liked. I was sprung, and everyone knew it. Trey knew it, but he never exploited me and, to my knowledge, never disrespected me.

We kicked it off and on. He was in his prime and living life as a single guy in college. When he canceled my visits, I would go anyway to cruise by his apartment. Sometimes I would see a woman's silhouette in the window. I stored the information for later use.

For over a year, we saw each other whenever possible. He was dating someone. I didn't care. I made myself available to him. The last time I saw him was a few months before my seventeenth birthday. I overheard my mom and Big Momma on the phone.

Momma wanted to move back to the country. If I had a chance with Trey, I needed to make a move. Maybe it was time he knew how much I wanted to be his main girl. So even if I left, I had something to look forward to when I came back to visit. He could even come to see me on holiday. I drove the two hours rehearsing what I was going to say. When I arrived, something unusual happened. The door was open slightly. I knocked anyway.

"Come in," Trey said.

"Your door is open."

"I heard you come up the stairs."

I walked in, and he closed the door behind me. Trey pulled me in and pinned me against the wall. He raised my arms with one hand while the other went down my pants. Switching hands, he searched for any lickable spot on my body. Suddenly he stopped.

"We need to talk."

"What's wrong?"

"Nothing's wrong. Let's go in the bedroom." Trey led the way. My stomach was in a knot. I had never seen him this way. His head hung a little low, and his speech was slow. We sat on the bed. I could tell he was

DownLow July 21 Thirsty

searching for the right words.

"Wassup, Boo?"

"I don't want to be Boo tonight."

Thinking he wanted to do some role-playing, I began to stand. "No, baby, please don't get up."

"Are you okay?" I said, sitting back down.

"Yes, I just want to look at you."

The moment felt too awkward for me to let it continue. I was unsure what he was about to say, but I knew I needed to say something first.

"Trey, I know I'm not the only one you see. I don't care. I want to be the only one."

"You are not ready for that."

"I'm serious."

"I like things the way they are, baby." He sealed it with kisses all over my face.

"Why am I the secret?"

"...Because my sisters and your mother would kill me. You know I'm that guy they all see as the one who goes around making babies," he said.

"No one just sees you as that."

"They do when it comes to me and you."

"I don't care what they say."

"I do. If I slip up with you, I must prove them wrong."

"What about how I feel?"

"Hey, shortie, this is getting too heavy. I'm single, and that's how it has to be. I'm Boo Jack."

I rolled him over and sat on his chest.

"You are so arrogant. Now try to get up."

"Lee, I'm trying to talk to you." He said with no attempt to move me.

"Baby, I'm in love with you. All right."

"So what's the problem?" I asked.

"I have obligations that make it hard for me to be with you like I want to."

I could hear the breakup rain coming down the track. The conductor was laying on the horn while the passengers prepared to get off at the next stop. I didn't want to hear him say it, so I did.

"It's cool, Boo. I'm good." I said, jumping up to leave.

He grabbed my hand, preventing me from walking away.

"Let me go, Trey. I need to go." I said, fighting back the tears. He loosened his grip.

"Please don't leave."

I wrestled him to the bed with me on top. I knew it was over, but I had to have the last stand.

"Then, stop with all of this extra. My mom is talking about moving, and you want to break it off with me."

"I'm not breaking it off." He said to my amazement.

"Okay, so what do you call it?"

"I was telling you how I felt. I don't know what to do, but I don't want to lose you. I can't see how this will work."

"You are confusing me," I said.

"I know. I'm fucked up too." He held my face close to his. I started to cry. He kissed away each one of my tears. I rested my head on his chest while he stroked my head.

"Lee," he whispered, "I love you."

I wanted to stay with him, but where could we go? Everyone was right. I was just getting started in my life and already in love with a man that had kids, baby Mamas, and a reputation as a womanizer. That was the backdrop for a lousy ending. I had to rewrite the script. He wasn't ending it, but there was no place to take it.

DADDY'S LITTLE GIRL

My dad was an absentee father from the time I turned thirteen. He was a Vietnam veteran and suffered from PTSD. Returning from the "conflict, " he had difficulty adjusting to civilian life. For four years, he knew nothing but to survive or die. He wasn't diagnosed, but it was evident to my mother and everyone who knew him before he enlisted that the war screwed him up. His drinking got worse after we left and moved to the city. She couldn't take any more of his verbal and borderline physical abuse.

From my mother, I've learned what it meant to love someone to death. She could not be with my father, but she never remarried. I witnessed abuse from him and I still loved him. He was just my dad, who was having a rough time, and I was his baby girl. He died before I graduated from college.

My home life was not dismal all the time when Dad lived with us. I had what I considered fun. Life was pretty good between playing dress-up and the family get-togethers every week. Playing dress-up with Dad's fatigues was awesome. A few times I wore them to school without permission. I had an hour to mess around before my parents came home from work. Fridays were the exception. I could potentially have two hours if my uncles had come over on Thursday. My dad loved to drink, and his weekend began on Thursday so he would buy his alcohol on Thursday. If my uncles had come over on Thursday, my dad would have had to go on Friday. He hated to go on Friday because most people did their alcohol runs on Friday.

On Friday, I was banking on them being late because my uncles had stopped by the night before. As I was about to put on the gun holster, I heard my parents in the driveway. I had forgotten my parents were going to a dance that night, and both of them had gotten off early. While putting his things back in his drawer, I stumbled onto what I knew to be a weed. All of my older cousins smoked. It was in a brown bag on top of some X-rated magazines: Playboy, Penthouse, Beaver Hunt, and Richard Pryor paraphernalia. That was my introduction to sex and drugs.

Lance Dickerson, my aunt's adopted son, became my hands-on experiment with this new information. I didn't touch the weed then, but I learned everything I thought I needed to know about sex from those books. I didn't go all the way with him with much of it. I wanted to save myself for someone special.

The summer before my senior year, my mom did move us back to the country. I had mixed feelings once I was back home. It was cool being with my friends from childhood, especially my best friend, Bridgette. When I wasn't fantasizing about Trey, I was trying not to visualize Bridgette. That girl could get me to do anything for her. I carried her books and did her homework. When she got accepted at LSU, and I was going to USD, I told her about my crush on her.

Bridgette stopped speaking to me for a long time.

When she finally talked to me again, she made ridiculous comments like, I forgive you for being a dyke. It's not your fault. She said it like it was some affliction.

I took her ignorance in stride. Besties can get away with stuff, and Bridgette was still a crush. Eventually, Bridgette's curiosities finally came to the surface. She started feeling me up on the sly. She would say she was playing but only did it when no one was around. When we hung out with our other friends, she stayed away. I cornered her in the locker room after school one day. She and I were the last two left after softball practice. I pulled her towel as she was coming out of the shower. She covered her body with her hands.

"Give it back." She screamed.

"Come and get it." I teased.

As she approached me, I popped her with the towel and dangled it in front of her.

"Come on, Lee."

She lunged for the towel and missed.

"You look like a pussy trying to get the string."

She lunged again, and I popped her with it again.

"Ouch, ma, stop."

That time she charged me and knocked me into the locker. We were fighting over the towel when we both heard a noise.

"Oh shit," We said at the same time. I let go of the towel as Coach Neale called out. "Is there anybody left?"

"Yes, ma'am," I said.

Bridgette used my distraction to grab the towel.

"Okay, lock the door when you leave."

"I will," I said.

Bridgette popped me with the towel.

"Ouch, B."

"Oh, it's not so funny now." She said mockingly. I pretended to be injured until she came closer. Then I jumped at her. Bridgette screamed as I chased her around the locker room.

"Okay, enough. I give up." She said, stopping short and forcing me to bump into her.

"You give up what?"

"You know." Bridgette put one leg up on the bench.

"I said, you know." She said again with a look in her eyes that I had never seen before. I had to dangle the carrot a little longer. She started rubbing her thigh on the inside. When she was close to her crotch, I said, "No." Her seductive eyes narrowed in disappointment.

"Why not?" She said.

"You are too funny acting. You don't want people to know you are feeling me."

"I'm not feeling you," Bridgette said, trying to be convincing.

"I can't tell," I said, looking directly between her thighs. Bridgette closed them and hopped down off the bench.

"I was just playing around." She said, grabbing up her clothes in embarrassment. I walked toward her, stopping short so she could bump into me.

"I get it. No one needs to know. But you don't have to act so funny when we are hanging out. You move away when I get near you." I moved closer. I could feel the heat from her naked body.

"People talk." She said. Her breathing was fast and deep. Our lips almost touched.

"You see, I can be close now, and you don't flinch. No one would ever suspect you wanted to get with me," I said.

She tried to kiss me. I turned my head.

"Too quick for you, slowpoke," I said.

"Come on, Lee. Kiss me." She said, trying to pull my face into hers. I held her back.

"Tell me you want me," I said.

"You know I do."

"Say it." She tries to kiss me again. Her lips brush against my cheek.

"Say it, Bridgette."

Bridgette put her leg back on the bench and pulled back her vulva.

"I want you." She said over and over again.

I gave her what she wanted and all of what I wanted. The whole time she was whispering. I want you. I agreed to keep our secret even though it would have been fine if people knew I had the hottest girl in the county sweating me. She decided to stop acting like I was a leper around other people.

No one ever suspected us. It did come close a few times. One time we played spin the bottle. When it was her turn, the bottle landed on me. The dare was for us to kiss. I gave her a wet sloppy tongue down her throat kiss. Bridgette tried to cover the awkwardness by pushing me away. No one cared. At other times she would sit by me and hug all over me. By then, we both had boyfriends, and I had other females interested in me. I was raised by a grandfather who said, "Don't let the right hand know what the left hand is doing." Bridgette wasn't serious about me, but I suspected she knew about the other girls and was jealous.

After prom night, Bridgette found out she was pregnant. Her guy was a contender for the number one seed NFL draft. She knew it was in her best interest to secure her future and stay with him. I felt some way about it, but she was my crush. I became her sidepiece. We had sex dates throughout her pregnancy. They tapered after the baby was born. By then, I was prepared for her to step in. I knew she would eventually go with him. He had the money, power, and prestige we all aspired to get. I was on the drill team. I had a girl at every high school in our district.

HATERS AND HYPOCRISY

While attending USD, I joined the ROTC. My father was my biggest hero. I planned to follow in his footsteps and become a marine. He did not like the idea at all. "The military has no respect for women." He would say.

"The times are changing, Dad". I said. "More women are becoming officers now. At one time, women could only be nurses. Now, we have female officers on the front line,"

"It doesn't matter." He said. "The rules will change, but people don't."

I knew he was right, but so was I. My mind was made up. He realized it. Seeing my determination which came from him he decided the best thing to do was get some of his buddies who were still active to look out for me.

"Dad, you taught me to follow my heart and my heart says go for it."

There was no use arguing about him having spies to check on me but I had to try.

"Dad, I want to do this on my own," I said without appearing argumentative.

"You will, but when shit comes up, and it will, I need to make sure you have some support on your six."

My dad would not say it out loud but he knew I liked girls. That was a big no-no in the military. He feared that my rebellious nature would get me caught up, but I knew letting anyone know I was anything other than heterosexual kept me alive. His fear almost came to fruition when I was in boot camp though

Patricia Burrell, a self-identified strictly dickly sister, tried to hem me up. She flirted with me, and I gave it right back. After we had sex several times, she said, "I'm not into girls like that."

This skank tried to ruin my career in the military by putting me on blast with another cadet. Little did she know, the girl she was telling was gay and had a crush on me. Patricia's final days in Bootcamp were hell. She was a private, and I was a Sergeant. It was on. I admit it was my fault for putting myself in that situation, but she violated my code. A person gets only one chance to screw over me. Patricia found it out the hard way. I hear she is still sleeping with everybody on her way to nowhere.

Life is good today. I'm dating this female named Tatiana. This girl is brown sugar with a pinch of cinnamon on a sticky bun. She is sweet and an actual ride or dies. Ironically, Tati and I dated the same guy at different times. She got pregnant, and the jerk denied it was his. At the time, she had no clue he was married. She kept seeing him even after he swore the kid could not be his child. Tatiana had a miscarriage at three months. He was back with his wife before she had a chance to grieve. It has been a while, but she still deals with it.

Honestly, I would not have dealt with Tatiana if I

had known about him initially. After Bridgette, I had a "no licking where he has been sticking" rule. I refused to carry baggage heavier than mine. The women I dated had to be lesbians. I feared getting with a woman who had guys running in and out of them all the time. Things started changing when I dated some self-identified lesbians. When the relationships were over, I discovered they had been or were still dealing with men secretly. That was a game-changer. Either I would give up women and just date men or try looking at everyone as an individual.

Tatiana entered my life at a good point. I was working through my issues. She had so many; mine was a piece of cake. But the best thing about Tati is that she's a femme on the street and a stud in bed. She surprised me with her strap-on and works it like it was attached. She feels me when I'm about to ejaculate, giving me the perfect amount of momentum with her push. I'm never left with a partial orgasm. She helps me ride it out. I give it right back. I believe this level of lovemaking keeps my dating pool full. Men and women love me and want to still be in my life even if we are not having sex. Trey is no exception, and he's back. I'm not sure if he can flow with my new program. I date whom I want, but I have sex with only one man and one woman at a time. Trey is not into the polyamorous life, but he says he could get used to anything for me. We'll see about that.

JUSTICE UNPLUGGED

The Power of Influence is not a tool or weapon to force someone into submission. Power of influence directly results from someone authentically being who they are and others seeing it and wanting to duplicate that authenticity in self. If used in any other way, it is manipulation. I can count on both hands and feet how many times I've tried to manipulate situations, only to have them backfire. I was often unaware I was doing it until someone pointed it out. As soon as I took my hands off the situation, the flames died out, and the resolution manifested. Prime example, I was on the rebound from the "Crash of 2007," my affectionate name for my ex was twice removed, and then I collided into a 10-car pile-up called Con (short for con artist), my ex once removed.

Con and I were planning our wedding after two beautiful whirlwind weeks of knowing each other. We skipped the U-haul and went straight to the altar. My healing from the "Crash of 2007" had only included three weeks of crying on a friend's couch, listening to India Irie's Journey to India, and affirming forgiveness. I thought I was over the embarrassment of losing all my possessions and dignity when I took a chance on a life with the Con. Three weeks were not enough to erase five years of a lie. I had to go deeper, but I did not know it would get so dark.

You see, the "Crash of 2007" and I was over long before I invested my savings into the dream of changing the world through music and free love with him. The goal was mine. Somehow he took over my dream, and it turned into a nightmare. I saw the signs of his deception. The proverbial eyes were wide shut to everything except what I wanted to see. I believed in following things through until all possibilities were exhausted. It seemed logical at the time. So much was already invested, and it was my dream. Yet, I found myself alone in a city I chose by default, and I couldn't breathe. Three weeks after that nightmare brought me back to ground zero, I bounced off my friend's couch and landed in the lap of Con.

My family disapproved of Con from the very beginning. My friends supported me, but they made it clear they were against me being with her. My father is a man of few words. He said a lot in a straightforward statement.

"You are daddy's baby, but you have lost your damn mind if you think I will condone this."

My mom had a lot to say.

"How long have you known her?" She asked.

"About a year," I lied.

"The engine is still hot from your Chicago exodus, and you are marrying a woman."

"What difference does that make, Mom?"

"You need time to get yourself together." She said.

"I'm good, ma."

"No, you're not."

"What's your problem? Why can't you be happy for me?" I pleaded. I just wanted her to support me.

"Why her?"

"Oh, I see. All of this pushing back is because she is a woman."

My mom threw her hands up to the sky.

"You are not hearing me. Justice, please don't do this."

With my mom's pleas and my dad's position, I perceived everything as a refusal to participate in my happiness because I was identifying as a lesbian. I set out to prove a point and become the poster child for the LGBT community. The state prohibition honoring same-sex marriage made me more determined to brandish my wedding/union all over the airwaves.

I created a stage play wedding ceremony. It was complete with costumes and lights, and a playbill. I sent out invites and invitations to family members who knew nothing of my sexuality. I hoped that they would call my parents. My parents would feel pressured to acknowledge me and give in.

My children and a few friends stood by me while holding candlelit vigils. They were hoping I would come through this dark period sooner than later. The entire time no one knew how much pain I was still suffering. My quest to suppress the past was to set a course to prove a point that was not the real point. I was broken, homeless, and feeling abandoned by God.

That was the real deal. I needed something to distract me from my pain. I was fighting for a cause that created that distraction. At the time, I did not know how much more it indeed was to whom I would later become.

Con knew my vulnerabilities. She fed on my insecurities. My dream to go to California became her campaign for getting me to be hers. I noticed her manipulative spirit and deceptive nature in other areas, but I didn't care. I had to show everyone that I may be a lesbian, but I could still make it in the world and have a relationship. I also thought I could help. I saw a beautiful spirit inside of her, but she needed to want it to live. She was another distraction.

The stage play of a wedding and public declarations of being a lesbian caused me to be out of communication with everyone who loved me.

There was nowhere else for me to turn except inside. Con was so insecure and jealous that I prayed she would turn the corner. Periodically, she would read my journal and attempt to make an issue out of something she read without me knowing the source. I started planting things for her to read. Items of a loving nature, hoping maybe it would help make our lives more pleasant. Nothing worked. I was so paranoid that I had begun thinking in secret.

California was a lonely place at first. I knew no one. Con told me she had many friends and a place to live. Those two factors sold me on us moving there within weeks of our union. I wasn't prepared to move so soon. I first wanted to line up employment, but I trusted Con. She knew no one, and we slept in the car the first night and then in a hotel for about a week. She scammed everyone we met, and I said nothing. I didn't know what to do. My life was screwed up, and God was not hearing me. But I cried to him anyway. That started the process for me to plan my escape from her. My need for survival would make me do many things, but I would not compromise my character. I let go of all I thought I needed to do and dropped to my knees. "God, I can't do this alone."

Within weeks, my life turned around. I reconnected with Source-God-Self. I reclaimed my power by accepting my imperfections and decisions even when they did not pan out as anticipated. My failures seemed more like opportunities to grow. They did not define my character as I once believed. I had let go of all of the shit that said I was not enough.

Four years later, I could finally talk to my parents about that time.

MOM

"When you would bring Trina and then Lisa around, I thought, okay, I'm not sure if she is gay or they are just friends. You allowed me to get to know them, and it didn't matter. Con came out of nowhere, and you had just had your heart broken by the Crash of

2007. You said you had known her for a while, but I knew that was a lie. When I finally saw her, I had to throw up my hands. I asked God to take care of you. You had to have lost your mind to be with that girl. She looked crazy as hell."

DAD

"When that woman asked me if she could have my grown daughter's hand in marriage, I wanted to throw her out of my house. Out of love for you, I didn't, but I prayed you would be okay every day. Something about her just wasn't right."

JUSTICE

"So this had nothing to do with me being bisexual?"

MOM and DAD

"No"

I understood. I had to go through that to reach a point where I could stand up and be okay in my skin. I thought I had been abandoned, but I was the one who had cut myself off. My challenges clouded the vision given to me long before I met The Crash of 2007 and The Con. My fears had crippled me, but my ego provided a path for me to heal. People say that pride is a sin and ego can hinder growth. I learned that my pride kept me from killing The Con, and my ego helped me walk away from The Crash of 2007 with my head held high. I was being prepared for the other bullshit that was yet to come when a person decides to take control of their own life. It was time for me to create the big picture from the snapshots.

Years have passed. Several family members have come to me and thanked me for opening their eyes to another way of seeing love. Most of my friends are cool with my open declarations of me. A few of them refuse to accept the diversity in the world, but I still welcome them with loving arms, and they stick around.

The Power of Influence I yield has momentum in the direction of change and uplifts all who dare to play with me, even if they disagree. Life is peaches and cream with a smidgen of raisins (I'm not fond of raisins, but they are suitable for me). The African

American bisexual woman, in her mastery of the art of Power of Influence, can use this critical component to elevate her knowledge of the Art of Selfishness.

The Art of
SELFISHNESS

TO ALIGN WITH SELF THROUGH A FEELING OR VIBRATIONAL AWARENESS, A CULTIVATION OF SELF

To discover the use of the ego to teach spiritual principles.

When it comes to sex, fear is a catalyst for silence and preserving ignorance. The stigma, slut-shaming, and curiosity-muting behaviors of ordinary people silence those who want to understand themselves and their bodies better. Desire is natural, but navigating the contemporary world of sex is an acquired skill. Thus, black women need to learn, teach, and inspire each other to embrace their sexuality, preserve their health, and live their best sex lives.
Arielle Loren(Clutch Magazine)

Isn't it ironic that sex, one of the most profound

spiritual connections we can share and a catalyst for giving life, has been used throughout history to take it away? It spawns creativity in every aspect of life.

There is nothing more delicious than the feeling one has when one makes love to another who is feeling that same deliciousness. Delicious sex is like my meditative process. I plan for it, prepare for it, pick a location for it, and make sure I have privacy. The latter is an option, And last, I go all in to let go and let God.

Picture In The Wallet

L ISA.

My spirit can't be contained.

Remember that last piece of sweet potato pie Big Momma baked for homecoming Sunday? It would be delicious, succulent, and satisfying to all the senses. Not too sweet and firm yet soft. And, no matter how much Big Momma said the pie was for the church, it tasted too sinfully decadent to be true. That is how I felt about Malik Asia, the first man I had ever met with an eight-pack. His abs were symmetric and perfectly placed on his long torso. He spoke three languages, including Swahili. When he had used all of them, I spoke in tongues. Oh my goodness, he was the epitome of a Mandingo warrior and hung like a tree. I don't need it to be big, but I like it. I just like things big and long.

My ex-girlfriend, crazy Kya, stood 5'11 with caramel skin. She had big lips and big thighs to match her big brown eyes. Her legs were longer than most days. After one night with her, my naturally curly hair was straighter than a Mizani Perm. I loved her big butt and her smile.

We met speed dating. That's when you sit across the table from someone for a few minutes, ask and answer questions, and then rotate to the next person. You report your interest to the coordinator at the night's end, and they play matchmaker. My best friend Trinity registered me to play and told me afterward. I had no clue what it was about, but Trinny knew I was still not dating, and neither was she.

"Have you played before?" I asked. "Many times," she boasted.

"How has that worked out for you?" "I met some cool people."

"I already know cool people. Any love connections?"

"A few, but nothing worked out," Trinny said.

"Exactly, so what's the point."

"The point is it's fun for you, and you meet people you may never meet."

"I do that on the internet all the time."

"What chat sites are you on?"

"I'm talking about meeting people in general, Trinny."

"How will you ever find someone if you hide behind your career and never get out?"

"I get out when I can. This school year is tough now that I am considering stepping down as Principal. Many things up in the air."

"You never go anywhere. I would know." She said.

"You don't know everything I do."

"I know you sleep with your cat because you can't get any other pussy."

"You are so silly. You need to stop being all up in my business."

"You brought me in. I would love to fall back." Trinny said.

"You are my memory. I need you." I said jokingly.

I stopped protesting and went. Trinny and I go way back. We stopped speaking for a few years because I thought she was too much in my business. My mother insisted Trinny was in love with me, but I knew it was just her being a busybody. She warned me about turning a booty call into a relationship, so we stopped speaking for about a year. The relationship with the booty call lasted five years, but in three of them, he repeatedly cheated until it ended with him sleeping with Trinny's girlfriend. She blamed me for it even though we both knew that was bullshit. She needed her friend back, and I needed her too.

We made up. After all, she was my rode cat. Friends like her are rare.

I put on my green power suit for speed dating. I'm a principal, but I get my sexy on. I spotted Kya right away. She had on the same dress, but it was smoking hot pink. I eased over to her side of the room and started a conversation. When I discovered it was her first time, I felt more comfortable being there. We decided to partner with each other for the first 5 minutes; then, we dipped into the bar. We hit it off immediately. Almost as fast as we met, we were a couple. I let her know I was bisexual before the first date.

"I don't get the bisexual thing. I think it's just confusion, but I am open to change if you can convince me."

I felt the hairs stand up on my neck. If I had a dollar for every time, I heard those words.

"Look, I said, you can have your opinion, but don't judge something you don't understand."

"Whoa, I respect that." She said, "Just promise me you won't dump me for some sweaty ass dude with hairy balls."

We laughed. I decided to let it slide, but something

said this moment would come back to haunt me, and it did.

Being a same-sex couple in California was colossal when Prop 8 was overturned. She asked me to marry her, and I said yes. We were making history. We decided to go with a salsa flash mob at the reception, but neither of us knew how to salsa. One of my Latino co-workers recommended her cousin.

Kya was excited about it until she met Juan Mendoza. Juan's stage name is Sexy Salsa Stud. Kya complained so much during our first lesson that I feared he wouldn't want to work with us again.

"Why can't we have a female instructor?" Kya asked.

"He is the only one that will do this for us without charging an arm and a leg."

"I don't like the way he touches me."

"Baby, salsa is a hands-on dance. It's sexy and sensual, but that is how it's supposed to be."

"He stares at you a lot."

"Come on now. We agreed. Don't do this?"

"I'm not doing anything. All right, but it's your fault if he feels me up." Kya was very serious. I could see it in her eyes.

"Go with the flow, baby. It's all good." I replied.

Kya did not make it easy for us to learn to dance together. It got to a point where she would only dance with me. I had danced salsa before, but not well enough to instruct. We got through it, but we were nearing the end, and I felt we needed to add at least one more session.

"I don't think we need any more lessons."

"Baby, I want it to be perfect for our day. I need more."

"I think you like Juan."

"Of course I do. He is an awesome dancer."

Kya advanced toward me. I wasn't sure what her intentions were. Her behavior had been very bizarre since we decided to marry. She stepped into my space.

"You want to get with him?" She asked, looking me dead in the eyes.

"No! And stop saying that."

"Why not?" She kept her stare.

"I'm with you."

"What if I give you my permission to sleep with him?" I turned to walk away. She grabbed my arm.

"No," I said emphatically, pulling away from her.

Kya's stare softened as if she was waking up.

"Why not?" She asked.

"First of all, your permission? You don't own me. And secondly, I'm not interested in multiple partners."

"I see how you light up when you are dancing with him. I can't help it. I'm jealous."

"Baby, I love to dance. You know that. Can we drop this other foolishness? I'm leaving town in the morning. Can we just go back to loving conversations now?"

Thankfully she agreed. I left the next morning feeling a little uneasy. I couldn't shake how threatened I felt around Kya. Her position with Juan was perplexing. Did she want me to sleep with a man? If so, why? One reason I was considering leaving my job as principal was to seek a career in theatre. I had become a little too complacent in academia and wanted something more. My trip was an audition for a significant part in an off-Broadway production. If I landed the role, I would resign as principal with the hopes of never turning back.

Kya greeted me at the airport with flowers and a sign that said, "Driver for a Superstar named Lisa." At home, there was a "Welcome Home" banner on the garage. A path of rose petals from the door to the bathroom ended in a jasmine-scented bubble bath. In our room, written on the mirror in red lipstick was, "I missed you." This is the Kya I adored. She loved surprising me, and I loved being surprised. Three days before our wedding, she sent me a text message. "Can you be home by 7?"

"Yes."

"Enter through the garage." She said.

"What's going on?"

"No questions. Trust me you will love it."

I love surprises so I could hardly wait to get home. When I entered the garage there was a note on the door, Put your things down in the living room. Take off everything except your bra, panties, and heels. Put the blindfold on. It's on the coffee table. Then, call out for me. After that, there will be no more talking.

I did as instructed. I felt her come up behind me. She slipped her arms around my waist before whispering, "Take my hand."

Kya guided me upstairs. I could smell frankincense and sage as we approached the top.

"Am I being sacrificed?" I asked jokingly.

"Shush. Watch your step."

Once we reached the top, I assumed we would take a left to our bedroom. She turned to the right toward the office. Kya removed the blindfold, and my mouth hit the floor. Juan Mendoza was in nothing but a bow tie and dance shoes. There were portable mirrors around the wall and a temporary dance floor in the middle. Our desk was pushed to one side and set up like an altar. Around each leg was a rope.

"Kya, what is this, and why is Juan here?"

"We had one more dance session. So, I thought it would be nice to do it here." "But why are we, me, him...."

"Nakedness removes the mystery. I know you've imagined him with his clothes off. And after talking to him, he has been having thoughts about you too."

I paused as Kya walked into view dressed in a black leather bustier and crotchless panty with thigh-high boots and a whip in her hand. I was uncomfortably aroused, but there was something different about her.

"Kya, baby, I appreciate that you want to do something special for me, but I'm not sure about this."

"You wanted me to loosen up a bit." She said.

"This is a lot more than what I was thinking."

"It's okay, Lisa. As you said, go with the flow."

"Kya has gone to some lengths to prepare for this day. Shall we dance?" Juan said. He hit play, and Kya presented me to him to dance. Both of them took turns dancing with me. I was spinning between them like a top. Kya looked like a professional. I was in awe of how much she had learned. On the last dance, Kya dipped me, and Juan picked me up. They both escorted me to "the bed." There was no talking.

Juan lay on "the bed." Kya pulled up the ropes tied to the legs of the bed and secured Juan. She poured baby oil over him and motioned for me to come over. We rubbed the oil over his entire body. Kya lingered around his penis.

"Lisa? Do you know what this is called?"She asked.

"Of course, it's a hand job," I said.

"That's a way to describe it, but I like the term fluffing better. It sounds more inviting. Here you do it."

Kya placed my hand under hers and continued to stroke Juan's penis.

"Put this cock ring on him." She said.

"When did you learn all of this stuff?" I asked.

"I told you she has put in some work to prepare for this night," Juan said.

Kya cracked the whip. "Stop talking." Juan replied, "Yes, mistress."

I was intrigued, so I stayed quiet. Kya climbed up on Juan. He slowly inserted his penis inside her. I was in shock watching her ride him like a professional. She cracked the whip on him a few times. Juan would go harder each time she did. My mouth hit the floor. In all the years we had been together, she had never been dressed like that, and she was taking dick. She swore she never wanted to have sex with a man again.

I watched them for about five minutes before she reached out to me. I joined the party. She got off, and I got on. An hour or so later, Juan left, and we lay in silence. Kya broke the silence.

"Did you like your surprise?"

"Yes, I'm confused, however. Why this? "

"You wanted to be with him. I could tell. I wanted to be the one to give you what you wanted instead of you sneaking off to get it."

"But you did him too."

"I had to tame him for you." She said with an air of indignation.

"It looked like you had done it before," I said.

"I've had some practice, and I've been watching some S&M." She bragged.

"The look on your face when you were riding him was priceless. You enjoyed it like you had been with him before."

"I knew it was only a matter before you would sleep with him. I tried him out first to see if he was worthy of you."

"Are you kidding me? You didn't do this for me." I screamed.

"Don't get upset with me. You are the one who said you wouldn't have sex with anyone but me, but you did it." She appeared to be basking in victory.

"You set this up so you could prove a point."

"Maybe I did." She said. Kya had no remorse.

"Unbelievable."

"I know you can be with someone other than me."

"This is not happening." I started to get up. Kya pinned me down hard.

"I'm okay, honey. I don't think I'll do it again. But I don't mind if you do."

I didn't say anything; The whole scene was

borderline crazy. I didn't know if I could trust a word from her mouth. There was more going on than I could put my finger on. I called her bluff and slept with Juan a few times because I was crazy. I said nothing.

The day I got the news that I had gotten the part, I rushed home to tell Kya. All of my clothes were packed in the middle of the floor. Kya saw me and started screaming about how much of a whore I was while throwing more stuff on the floor. She had been monitoring my text messages and found out about Juan. It had been several months since I had seen him. She called me every name in the book except the child of God.

"I wasn't serious about you fucking him."

"That is not what you said, and you fucked him too!"

"That was for you."

I stopped talking. All I kept thinking was this is crazy. I knew we were coming to an end after that night. The respect I had for her was done. We were over, and I never looked back. I never saw Juan again, but she was spotted with him around town. This is where my piece of sweet potato pie enters the picture.

Malik and I were both casts in a production of A Raisin In The Sun. We flirted from the beginning. The director hated fraternizing, so we were very discreet when we started seeing each other for more than rehearsal. I was on the rebound, Malik would only be in town for the run of the show, and he lived an eight-hour plane ride away. It seemed safe enough to play a bit.

The production had a six-week run. The actors would have a week's break in between. Malik said he needed to take a trip home during his break. The night before he was scheduled to leave, we hooked up for some traveling sex. Just as my pinky toe was uncurling, Malik decided to confess. "I'm married."

I almost choked on my saliva. "Damn, did you have to tell me this now?"

The arch in my back finally flattened. I waited for him to say something. Instead, he grabbed his wallet, and the money fell out.

"Are you fucking kidding me?"

"No, it's not like that." He said, picking up the

money. "Here," he pulled something from his wallet and handed it to me.

"This is my wife."

I was in shock. Is he giving me a picture of his wife? I had thought of punching him, but I took the picture without saying a word. I stared at it for a minute before saying anything. A part of me wanted to be angry, but I couldn't. Something about the moment humbled me.

"She's beautiful." I couldn't believe I was saying it, but I did.

"We've been through infidelity on both sides. I promised her I wouldn't do it again."

I handed back the picture. For some bizarre reason, I didn't punch him in the face. I wasn't even mad.

"Why did you do it?"

"I like you. I'm attracted to you. All the things that make anyone want anyone, but I can't get her off my mind."

"I guess not now that you will be seeing her tomorrow. Right?"

"That's true. I love my wife, but I want to be with you too."

He continued to talk, and I listened. The average sister would have cussed him out and kicked him out. I wanted to, but something compelled me to keep listening. When he apologized to me, he was more apologetic for forgetting about her than the fact that he had played me. Somehow that made him more attractive to me. When I told Trinny, my Jersey girl switched on.

"Where is this asshole so I can cut off his dick and shove it down his throat?"

"Trinny, it's not that serious."

"Like hell, it isn't What kind of man would do something so disrespectful? You can't let him get away with that. Let's call her."

"Not... She knows he cheats."

"What the hell do you mean? This is to get back for how he treated you."

"I agree that it was not the way I would have preferred to find out, but something in the way he talked about her...."

"What is wrong with you? He was thinking about his wife while he was doing you."

"I know, Trinny. I was there."

"Then why are you giving him a pass? This is not the Lisa I know."

"Listen. My days of fighting over a man ended days. It was a long time ago. I'm a warrior princess on my way to being the queen of somebody's universe."

"I don't think his castle is big enough for two queens and this ass-kicking. Girl, he is a married man who shows off his wife's picture in the middle of sex. He's a dog who should be castrated. Don't they do that in Africa?"

"It wasn't in the middle of sex. It was at the end, and he lives in Chicago. But that is not important."

"Okay. What is the point?"

I found out before I started catching feelings, and when he talked about his wife, Malik had a look of reverence on his face. I saw his love for her. Here he was in another woman's bed. He just finished having sex and is giving his wife her props.

"Lisa, you are doing that tree hugger thing again. Break it down for me." Trinny said, looking like a deer in headlights.

"Malik could have told me before, but he didn't."

"That would have been a deal breaker, and you know it," she said.

"Maybe, maybe not. It was just sex, but before that night, I wanted to be somebody's queen. I had no clue what that looked like. Kya called me her queen, but she had little regard for who I was. I was in the palace on the throne with all the attention and the trinkets, but that was all for her. Malik carries his wife in his heart and his wallet. That is the point. I don't want to be a queen as a symbol. I want to be the picture in the wallet and on the cell phone, and the damn screen saver."

"Lisa, you need to get out more. All this talk about queens and thrones. I've been invited to a bisexual meetup. It's a new group, but it sounds exciting. You wanna go?" Trinny said, still looking like a deer in headlights.

199

"Listen, Trinny. Kya had me wondering if loving that intensely was worth the risk."

"Kya set you up, and the bitch was crazy."

"Yes, but I went for the bait when I wanted to be the picture in the wallet all along."

"Are you saying you would be okay with your partner having sex with someone else as long as they have your picture?"

"No, dang Trinny, you don't get it."

"You are right, but as long as you get it, then I'm good. I don't know. Let's get a few drinks, then maybe I will see the light. And then, we can go to Chicago to kick Malik's fine ass."

Ride or Die

IMANI.

Hi, I'm Imani and I'm an emotional vampire"
That's how I would have introduced myself a few
years ago. I've been extremely clingy, needy, and
insecure. I drove myself crazy. I was about to hire me to
treat me. I'm a life coach. I am certified to help you
undress your mess while I clean up mine. No one helps
another at random. It is a win-win situation. My son
has special needs. And I had to maximize my earnings
to accommodate his medical bills, so I went back to
school to study engineering.

I love me some Candace. We are societal wrongs on
so many levels: two women, an interracial couple
(republican and Democrat, catholic and Baptist), and
Candace is my fiancé's twin sister. It's complicated.

CANDACE

We happened way too fast. In the beginning, it was a simple flirtation with a few words and glances here and there. My brother Gary introduced me to Imani. I liked her from the first hug. After we exchanged numbers, texting quickly advanced to sexting. We progressed to phone sex which was ideal considering my hectic schedule.

Imani is raising a male child without the help of his father. My mother did the same after my father died, except she came with the addition of a gay daughter, which has endeared me to any woman who managed without having someone to help. My brother sidestepped many of the trappings of what society creates for the African American male, like teen pregnancy, drugs, and fast money. Our mother never eased up on him. Gary did have other trappings that got him into sticky situations. His arrogance made it difficult for him to make friends.

For some ungodly reason, he had a strange sense of entitlement, as if someone owed him something. Our mother would have none of it. She made us earn everything without expecting a reward. "Your reward comes when you have given your best," she said.

Imani's sperm donor wanted nothing to do with their son, Josiah. The sorry asshole wanted Imani to have an abortion. When she refused, he punched her in the stomach. He abused her mentally and physically. Imani had a standard delivery, but Josiah is autistic. His special needs are challenging, but she has provided top-tier care.

Imani and I became intimate for the first time at a club. It wasn't until later that same night that we made love. She tried hard not to show her vulnerability and fear. Josiah's father's physical abuse created a barrier to her ability to enjoy sexual contact. I took my time with her, and she opened up like a precious flower. She did try to put on her poker face until her orgasms started. She started crying.

"What's wrong?"

"This is a first."

"Did I hurt you? I'm sorry."

"No, I've never had an orgasm."

"Seriously?"

"Does it look like I'm joking?" She said.

I had noticed the tears and the shaking, but that is what I do. However, Candace advanced to sobbing.

"Oh wow, I'm sorry. I didn't mean it like that. I'm glad it was with me." I said. Making love with her was very gentle. I could tell there was a lion inside of her waiting to come out. One of my faults with sex is that I go all and pull out inhibitions. I've been told you should never do that in the beginning. I can't do it. Being a woman's first anything is an instant commitment to something. I had no idea I would fall for her. We progressed fast. Then things started getting messy. It was inevitable.

On average, I sleep in my bed four times a month, and they are only sometimes consecutive. Imani expects me to be available every time she calls. Some days I work twelve hours with limited breaks. It's the life of a spokesmodel. When I take a break, I have to go to makeup, or I'm prepping for the next shoot. Imani expects me to answer her every call. I finally set a daily reminder to call her. The first time I missed my reminder alarm, she called the hotel

I was staying in and left several messages. I called as soon as I got it, but she had already gone ballistic. I couldn't take it anymore. There was strong potential for a disaster. It had to end.

WHEN IMANI MET GARY

"Is this how you pick up women?" Imani screamed while banging on the hood of Gary's car.

"Only the ones I plan to stuff and keep." He retorted.

"Really?" She said in astonishment.

"Where are you headed? Maybe I can give you a lift." Gary asked. Imani looked at him as if he had three heads.

"Are you serious? You almost ran me over. Now you offer me a ride. What's next? Are you going to throw me in the back seat and ask me out to dinner?"

"I would love to." He said mockingly.

Imani was annoyed and flattered by his assertiveness and wit. "Is that the best you can do?"

She asked.

"Oh, you want more. That's going to cost you extra."

"It never stops, huh?" I chuckled.

"Not for you, and I got you to smile. That should be worth at least lunch."

"Imani walked away glancing back with eyes that said maybe. Gary jumped out of the car and walked behind her. "Where I'm from when a person says maybe that's one step away from yes." Imani kept walking,

"And where I come from," she said," Maybe is just maybe." Gary caught up to her and handed her his card. "If you want to improve upon perfection, call me."

"Oh, I need improving." She said.

"No, I do."

Gary was so charming and assertive. The light changed as I crossed the street. I could feel his eyes following the sway in my hips because I solicited his attention. I turned to look back. He held up a piece of paper that read, "Call me."

I practically skipped the rest of the way to work.

"This is a first." Officer Woods said as I entered my office building.

"I've been working here for ten months, and this is the first time I've seen you smile."

"I smile all the time."

"I've never seen it." Said, Officer Woods. "It looks good on you."

"Thank you," I said, thinking about the last time I remembered smiling. I came up with nothing. Had it been that long? When did I get too busy to laugh? I work for the Department of Defense, which explains part of it, but I was voted class clown. Making me laugh was a requirement for potential dates. I especially liked the self-deprecating jokes. They exposed vulnerabilities that are necessary components to genuinely being accessible and authentic. Gary had me from the start. I didn't have to give him my list of what it took to be with me. He instinctively knew and held nothing back.

After two years of dating, Gary got me to say yes to marriage. Before him, I never saw marriage in the cards for me. The world applauded marriages lasting ten, twenty, or thirty years as a benchmark of achievement. My parents and their generation are examples of how longevity in marriage can be filled with years of unhappiness. That made it unattractive for the watchful observer. I was that observer.

Gary's treatment opened me to the potential for a different reality.

"If it doesn't work," he said, "at least you get great parting gifts," Gary said jokingly.

All jokes aside, marriage was sacred and not to be taken lightly for Gary. His father instilled that belief in him at an early age. He believed a man's worth was measured by his family. "A man with a strong family is a man people will respect and admire." He would say. Gary took his father's words as an obligation. It became the benchmark for all of his life decisions. He often pushed so hard to live up to that, that he would become depleted in other areas. He aimed to exceed expectations even when good enough was enough. Not a bad quality, except its void of celebrating the wins with the potential of overshooting the goal and missing out on the journey.

When Gary was only fifteen, he and his father were involved in a head-on collision. Gary survived, but his father didn't. His father's death left Gary with a huge void and survivor's guilt. Gary wanted to fill his father's shoes as his retribution for not dying that day. His mother, Mama Re, saw how troubled he would get when he didn't quite succeed. "Son, you cannot improve upon perfection," she would say. "However, you should never settle for it either." She wanted him to learn that he could never duplicate his father's life, which seemed perfect to Gary, but he could build upon his legacy by defining his strengths. Mama Re tapped into his passion for football and groomed him in that direction. That passion took him to the NFL. A knee injury ended his career before it barely began. The doctors gave him the option to play for another two to five years on a busted knee and escalate the deterioration, or he could quit and slow down the process considerably. Quitting was not an option, so he continued to play.

After a winning season that took them to the Super Bowl, he decided to retire on a high note. Never short on passion, Gary left the field but not the game. He continued his studies and earned his degree in orthopedic surgery specializing in Sports Medicine and Arthroscopic Surgery. Gary Birch, MD, patches up the athletes he once injured as a linebacker.

WHEN IMANI MET CANDACE

Candace went to college on an athletic scholarship.

Just like Gary. One of her goals was to go to the Olympics. After achieving that, she was approached by Fit Magazine to be one of their spokesmodels. A very shrewd businesswoman, she entered a lucrative agreement that afforded her resources in developing her own company Candi Consulting, LLC, which helps athletes build their brand from concept to creation and transition from athlete to entrepreneur. Candace donates her services to athletes in third-world regions around the globe. Tanzania is where she had been the day Gary and I picked her up from the airport.

The airport was chaotic as usual. Gary jumped out of the car to use the bathroom while I circled a couple of times. The flight was delayed, but we didn't see the alert until we arrived. I circled twice before he came out. I noticed Candace walking a few paces behind me as he walked toward me. She was talking on her cell, peeking from under a hoodie. I recognized her immediately. She is more beautiful than I had imagined. I've seen her pictures; she and Gary are identical twins.

"Candace this is Imani. Imani this is Candace."

"I'm a hugger." She said.

"I'm a hugger too." I mimicked, quickly jumping out of the car. I didn't know a hug could mean so much.

"I've heard so much about you, Imani. I'm looking forward to getting to know you better." She said.

Candace gave me the universal lesbian hug with an extra squeeze. Even though it felt like an invitation to more than sisterly bonding, I decided to interpret it as such anyway.

"It looks like you and I will spend time together."

"Wow, sis, I haven't told her yet."

"Told me what?" I said.

"Baby, I do listen," he said. "You have been complaining about getting ten pounds off before the wedding."

"Right..."

"And you want to shake up your career, right?"

"Yes."

"Believe me. I think you are perfect just as you are, but because I listen, I wanted to give you what you said you needed."

"Okay, Gary, spit it out," I said, oblivious to where he was heading.

"Candace will help you get off the ground with both."

I almost hit the floor. Candice Birch will be training me. Oh my God!

"I'm your one-stop shop." She said, beaming her signature smile I had seen many times in family photos, fitness magazines, and TV.

"Wow, I don't know what to say."

"All you gotta do is say yes."

Candace's voice echoed like Floetry. I was speechless, but I managed to say, "Absolutely. I need all the help I can get."

"Trust me; it will be easy for you. You are already in great shape." Candace looked at me from head to toe.

"That's what I keep telling her," Gary said, pulling me in for a kiss.

"I've hit a plateau," I said.

"We all do. Your body will respond quickly." She

said, looking at me up and down again. Gary pulled me in closer as if he was trying to shield her stares.

"Can you believe this body is about to be Mrs. Gary Harris?" It sounded like a question, but Gary was making a statement.

"I'll drive," Gary said.

"You can ride shotgun," I said to Candace.

"No, that is reserved for you, Mrs. Gary Harris." She said, jumping in the back seat. I detected a hint of sarcasm.

"Correction, Imani Saint James Harris," I said, winking at Gary. "Don't get it twisted."

"Gary, I think I like her already," Candace said, touching me on the base of my neck. I shivered a little. Gary placed his hand on my knee. "Are you cold, baby?" He asked.

"No, I'm good."

I could see Candace in the side view of the w mirror. I avoided her stare.

"Your brother's humor is rubbing off on me."

"I see."

Gary kissed my hand, " I love me some of you."

"Get a room," Candace said.

"Speaking of rooms." Gary said, "Are you going to Mama's or staying at Tiffany's?"

"You know I'm not with her anymore." She said with slight irritation.

"I thought maybe you had reconciled."

"Gary, why would you even ask me about her?"

"My bad sis! I thought time would have healed all of that." He said.

"Let it go, Gary!"

Candace's beautiful smile turned to stern indignation. Whatever happened with Tiffany, she was not happy with Gary reminding her. We rode in silence for a brief moment. Candace broke the silence with a joke. Gary followed suit, and it was as if the moment had never happened. I surmised that humor was how they both dealt with uncomfortable situations and laughed a lot.

The driveway was full of unfamiliar cars when we arrived at Mama Res.

"Mama has called the entire family," said Candace.

"And you know this," Gary replied.

"Imani, my family, hasn't seen me for a while, so it is about to get so loud we may not speak tonight. Let's connect in the morning to start our workout regimen. We will do two a day."

"Huh?" I said with a hint of fear in my voice.

"No worries, kiddo," she said, placing her hand on my arm. The chill returned, and she stroked it away. "It's just a split with cardio at one time and strength training at another. We need to trick the muscles a little bit."

"Okay," I laughed."Thanks for clearing that up."

"Absolutely," she said.

"Sounds good. Josiah will be with his grandparents until the wedding. We can begin tomorrow." I said.

"Josiah?" she asked.

Gary interjected, "Josiah is Imani's son. I told you about him over the phone."

"You did." She said.

"I did." He replied, getting the luggage out to the

trunk.

"You did not. You only think you did." Candace barked back, exiting the car. Mama Re walked up with family members in tow.

"Cut it out, you two. Candace, the baby, come give Mama some love."

Candace winked at me as Mama Re, and everyone else swarmed around. "Eagerness is welcomed, kiddo, tomorrow?" She said.

"Tomorrow."

Anxiety about the training kept me up all night. Candace was flirting with me, and I liked it. That was way too weird for me to even have in my head. I needed to shake it off. I took a long hot bath and talked myself into the fact that the attraction was only because they were twins. Those thoughts helped me through that night. However, they would wane as she and I spent more time together. I had no clue how crazy things were about to become.

One day of training with Candace felt like a week. I wasn't new to the gym, but Candace was an Olympian. Her idea of pushing through boundaries meant doing ten more of everything. My idea was to do two and a possibility of maybe one exercise.

"Come on, you can do it," she kept saying.

"Yes, I can, but will I be able to do anything else?" I responded, trying to gasp in between breaths. Without saying a word, she held up five fingers. At one point, I wanted to punch her, but she was too damn adorable.

Working out with Candace was excellent and challenging for a couple of reasons. I had difficulty concentrating when she assisted me with stretches and lunges. Every time she touched me or corrected my posture, I imagined some scene like us lying in a hammock on some remote island, feeding each other strawberries dipped in chocolate. The other reason is that she does not have an on-and-off switch. I only wanted to get in shape for my wedding, not train for the Olympics. Candace was working the hell out of me in more ways than one. Two weeks into our training, she had to go to New York for a one-day shoot.

"Darn, no training for three days. How will I survive without you?" I welcomed the break but would not see her for at least two to three days. As soon as the thought registered, I tried to delete it. I shouldn't be thinking about her like that. I was finishing my last set of 15 when she announced.

"You're going with me,"

"Really?" I said with the enthusiasm of a child going to an amusement park.

"I got to keep my eye on you. Give me five more." She said with a wink. "Plus, we can do some shopping for the honeymoon."

"Gary hasn't told me where we are going."

"Knowing my brother, it will be warm. That's a good place to start."

"True, okay, I just need to ensure I have coverage at work, and it's on," I said hesitantly. I enjoyed being around her on the home front. I would now get to see her in her element. I could hardly wait.

Before we arrived, Candace found out the shoot would not require much prep. Her friend was shopping for gigs with star power. Having Candace in her portfolio would give her more clout as a photographer. Candace was a natural. In the studio, I watched in awe how her beauty lifted the entire set.

Candace's inner beauty came through so clearly. Watching the process of makeup and hair was fascinating. I wore makeup but could never quite get it right. Finding the proper lighting and angles was crucial to a good shot. Her friend suggested we do some shots together.

"You two look like the perfect sexy lesbian duo." She said.

"I'm not sure that is a good idea with me marrying her brother," I said.

"It's only art, a fantasy." Candace offered.

"I didn't prepare," I said, trying to push back on such a crazy idea.

"Hook her up with some concealer and bronzer. Also, give her a new outfit." Candace said to the stylist.

In an instant, everyone went to work on me. I was so excited to be on the set with Candace. It was the best fifteen minutes of fame I could have ever imagined.

"You are a natural," Candace said. "The camera loves you."

"I bet you say that to all the girls," I said mockingly.

"Only when it's true." She replied with a kiss on the lips. I took a deep breath and let it go. It was nothing. People kiss on the lips in many cultures. I know it was one of those kisses. I wanted it to mean more.

The day was fantastic. I loved the aura that existed around Candace. Her spontaneity was captivating to everyone. I was caught up in her intoxicating energy like everybody else—no big deal.

The shoot lasted the entire day. I hadn't noticed until we exited the building.

"Wow. It was dark when we arrived, and now it's dark again." I marveled.

"Welcome to my world," Candace said as our car arrived.

"There will be no time for shopping today, kiddo. We'll do that tomorrow. It is time to unwind."

"Are we going to hit the gym while we are here? I feel like I'm cheating." I said.

"No one comes to New York to go to the gym. They

come to show off what they've been doing in the gym."

"I'm not sure I'm there yet."

"Are you saying that with all the work we have put in, you are still unhappy with your body?"

"No, I'm just saying I have more work to do."

"I'm your trainer. You trust me?"

"Yes."

"Cool," she said, pushing me into the car. "Driver, take us to 281 West 12th near 8th Avenue. This woman needs to let New York see what I see."

Three shots of peach Ciroq and I had no concerns for inches. Candace assured me that my training would not be hindered. She knew practically everyone in the club. She introduced me to her friends as her girl. While we sat at the table, she placed her hand on my leg several times. It felt nice until I gave it a thought. At that point, I would move.

Yet, I wanted her to keep doing it. She would look at me and smile. She had me hook, line, and sinker. I felt I would lose control at any moment, and she would reel me in. Unfortunately for me, around Candace, control was a facade.

"Come on, let's dance." She said, leading me to the dance floor. I let her walk several paces ahead of me. She twerked as she walked. The left cheek past the right one, and the bounce sent a ripple across the dance floor. I couldn't stop looking at her ass. As if on cue, the DJ played, There Goes My Baby, by Usher.

Candace turned to me and extended her hand. The closer I got to her, the faster my heart beat. Her breast was peeping out of her fitted top. I knew I was done. No turning back now. I wanted to kiss her so badly. I doubled over in pain when I was about to do it. "Oh shit!" I screamed." Bathroom!"

Candace grabbed my hand and maneuvered to the bathroom through the crowded dance floor.

Before I could close the door to the stall, I threw up for what seemed like an eternity. Candace held my hair back until it appeared I was done.

"Are you okay?" She said, handing me some paper towels.

"I think so. I'm a lightweight when it comes to drinking."

"Now you tell me."

The bathroom girl hands me a wet towel. "Here you go."

"Thank you."

"I'm used to it. Girls are drinking and can't hold their liquor. Did someone slip you something? I have something for that too." She said.

"There's a lot of that going on."

Her sales pitch was making my head spin more than the alcohol. Candace noticed and intervened.

"Could you please just give us some mouthwash?"

"Use a lot of this stuff too. It's the good kind, and it tastes great. I have some gum, mints, toothpaste…."

"The mouthwash will be enough," I said.

"Can you do us a quick favor?" Candace asked.

"Sure."

"My husband is waiting for us outside the door. Can you tell him we'll be right out?"

The bathroom girl hesitated. "I need to stay in here. I have many products."

Candace handed her a twenty.

"Okay." The bathroom girl took the money. As soon as she cleared the door, Candace locked it behind her.

"What are you doing?" I said.

Candace didn't say a word. I was sitting on the sink in two moves, and she was undressing me. She tried to kiss me, but I turned my head.

"Candace, I just threw up."

"And I just cleaned you up." "But what about...?"

She holds my face close to hers. Her gaze is soft and inviting.

"What about what?" She kissed me hard.

She leans down and licks around my nipples before biting them.

"Ouch."

Softly she looks into my eyes. "Do you want me to stop?"

"No."

I shoved her head between both breasts. She flicked her tongue across my left nipple, making the right one jealous.

The bathroom girl was banging incessantly,

"Open the door. What are you doing in there?"

"Candace, we should stop," I said not so convincingly.

"Why?"

Candace pulled me to the edge of the sink. She hoisted my legs up and used my hands to hold them open. I thought she was about to bury her face deep. Instead, Candace stepped back and unzipped her pants. I almost fainted. Candace had the most enormous cock I had ever seen on a guy, much less attached to a strap.

"What are you going to do with all that?"

Before I could protest any further, she shoved it inside of me. The marble was cold on my ass, but when our bodies touched, it became an inferno. I screamed so loud that the pounding on the door was muted. With quickness, Candace forced me over and entered me from the back. I screamed again. The pounding on the door became a chorus of fists, shouting, and chaos. All of a sudden, she stopped, and we both started laughing.

"This is security; I'm coming in."

"Oh shit," we said at the same time. We started scrambling to get our clothes back on. We managed to get it together within seconds of the security guard opening the door.

"Is everything okay? I heard screams." He said. I grabbed my hand. "The water was too hot," I said.

The bathroom girl was looking over her things on the sink and cussing under her breath. "Hot water, my ass." We had disrupted her counter store. Her products were in disarray. The lotion was spilling onto the floor.

"You may want to get that fixed before someone is seriously injured," Candace said.

"Let me take a look," said the security guard.

Candace grabbed my hand and rushed me out of the bathroom as she rushed me in. We whisked past the crowd that had formed outside the door and bolted for the exit. We jumped into a taxi and sped off.

"I didn't see that coming," I said

"With me, you never will."

Candace was easy to be with. When we were apart,

I couldn't wait for the next moment. Even if she was in the next room, I anticipated seeing her as we passed one another. The glances, the rendezvous' at my house, and any place we could steal a moment.

For once, I felt alive. Candace was all I could think about. It was easy to love someone like her, but I was engaged to her brother. I wondered if I was being selfish and allowing passion to take over my common sense. I needed to talk it over with Candace, but she worked hard. Some days I worked out by myself.

After a while, the guilt subsided, but my anxiety increased. I didn't plan any of this. It just happened. Candace was my first woman, but I did not want to find another. It would be easy if it were someone other than my fiancé's sister.

How could Candace respect me and want me if I was cheating on her brother with her? I wanted to be with him and her sexually. That idea was too weird, so I put some distance between him and me. I just said I wanted it to be fresh for the honeymoon. It was hard. Things began to unravel inside me and on the outside. I dropped the ball on the wedding. Once I let myself calm down, I decided to call off the wedding.

Candace was only sometimes available. I could never get her alone or on the phone long enough to put it in perspective. When I called, she could never call me right back. Sometimes it would be a whole day before I heard from her. After two long days of not hearing from her, I hit a boiling point. I couldn't keep my composure. There was much screaming with very little real listening on my end.

"It's over… I'm done…" she said. The world stopped on its axis. For some ungodly reason, I needed to hear it again."What did you say?"

"It is over, Imani."

"Noooo."

"I can't do this anymore." She said.

"Do what?"I screamed.

"The arguments and the constant calls when I'm working. I can't give you what you want."

"All I want is you."

"You say that, but with me come many lonely nights. It would help if you had more than that. Gary is what you need. You need security."

Oh my God, I couldn't let her slip away. I started begging.

"I'm okay with your schedule, baby. I just needed help with the right way to call the wedding off."

"Call off the wedding? No, you can't do that," she shouted.

"I can't marry him. It's not fair to him or me."

"You're confused. It's my fault. You can make it work with him." "What the hell do you mean I'm confused?"

"Imani, you and I won't work. Gary adores you. He can be there in ways I can't."

"My mind is made up, Candace. I'm going to talk to Gary and tell him the truth. Then, you and I can be in the open." I said.

"That won't happen," she said

"What? Why?"

"You don't know me, Imani. I'm not a good person."

"What are you talking about? I see how you work

in the community. You are a role model."

"That's all a facade. I'm backstabbing my brother. A good person does not do that."

"Backstabbing? This just happened. We didn't plan it. We need to come clean." I pleaded.

"I did plan it," she blurted out.

"What does that mean?" The walls started closing in.

"Getting with you was supposed to be payback. There you go. I've said it."

"Payback?" I said incredulously

"Gary slept with my first girlfriend when we were in high school. He said he didn't know I liked her, but I didn't believe him. Everybody knew, including her."

"You're lying."

"Imani, I'm sorry, but it's true."

"This is some bullshit."

"He deserves to be happy."

"You got with me to get back at your bother for some teenage bullshit. I don't care. I know you love me. And you want me to forget about you and be with

Gary because he deserves happiness? What's wrong with you? So do we."

"Marrying him is better for all of us. I got to go."

"Candace, please don't hang up." I pleaded with her over and over. The phone went silent.

"Hello," I said.

"I'm here." She replied.

"We can make this work. I've just been a little stressed lately. Look, let's have a do-over. I love you." After a long silence, she said, "Imani, I'm sorry, but I don't love you."

I couldn't believe what I was hearing. Neither of us had ever uttered those three words in all the time we had been together. Not even in the heat of the moment when we were having sex. Yet, in one instance, we were using them in opposite ways. My heart broke into a million pieces, but I couldn't give in to it. My ego would not allow me to give her the satisfaction of my tears. She started to speak again.

"Don't say another word," I said.

I yelled several obscenities before finally hanging

up. My head was pounding. The wedding was only a month away. Our bridal party brunch was jumping off in a few days. What was I going to do?

The day before the brunch, I had calmed down considerably. Something inside of me could not believe Candace meant what she had said. Either way, I needed closure. I had to try one more time. I invited Candace to come over after the bridal luncheon. She agreed to come. I wasn't ready to let go, so I planned how I would seduce her. I figured she would be walking away if she didn't love me. We could start fresh if I were right; she didn't mean it.

In the meantime, Mama Re was putting the finishing touches on the luncheon. She wanted everything to be perfect for her baby boy. Mama Re took over the planning of all the details. Her grandiosity spared no expense. I was too preoccupied to care that her ideas were far above what Gary and I wanted.

The drive to Mama Re was excruciating. I was a nervous wreck. Candace and I had not seen each other since the phone call. It would be the first time I would be in the room with her and Gary at the same time in weeks. Candace's text broke the grip.

"Mama's asking questions about us hanging out so much. Be Prepared."

As if I didn't already have enough stress. I knew Mama Re was watching my every move. She told me the first time I met her. "Under no circumstances will I see my heartache and not do whatever it takes to get rid of the pain," she said. "Gary is my heartbeat, young lady. Believe what I say."

It was the way that she looked at me that told the story. A look I had seen in the mirror when I hit my son's father with a baseball bat after I got off the floor after he tried to kill our son and me. Gary assured me her bark was louder than her bite.

However, I knew she still had a bite. She had asked me things about myself that could have only come from postings on Facebook. She admitted she had googled me after Gary told her I was recognized for working in S.T.E.M education in primary and secondary schools. Facebook gave her the rest of my story; college education had never been married, had one child owned my home, and was the byproduct of a two-parent family. I deduced that her inquiry should not be taken lightly.

By the time I arrived, I was as ready for Mama Re. I concluded my best course of action would be to say very little, look shocked at her questions, and convince her nothing was going on. I knew it was deceitful considering the truth, but I would have no chance of winning without Candace on board to support the fact. If I could pull it off, it would be a miracle. Many thoughts were taunting me, but for today, they needed to take a back seat. Candace and I would play the perfect sisters-in-law-to-be, period. Gary would be there, so I had to make it work.

The luncheon was a huge success. Mama Re outdid herself with the food and the ambiance. The tension between Candace and me resurfaced a few times, but her jovial nature helped me brush it aside. She has a sense of humor that rivals the best standup comics. A quality she and Gary share. He was glowing like he was the bride. Even my father, whose emotional default setting is grumpy, appeared to enjoy himself.

All of my preparation and anticipation of an uncomfortable dialogue with Mama Re seemed unnecessary as the evening came to a close.

Everybody began saying their goodbyes. My parents and the rest of the wedding party were already out the door. I was eager to get home to wait for Candace's arrival. I looked around for her to confirm the night, but she had disappeared. Gary and I headed for the door. Mama Re called out to me from the other room. "Imani, can you stick around for a bit."

"Ma, Imani and I are planning to catch an early movie tonight," Gary said, winking at me. His attempt to save me from his mother didn't work. She met us at the door.

"It will not take that long, son." She said.

"Okay, Mama Re," I said, looking at Gary.

"You can go to the movies another night. I have some last-minute wedding details to take care of, Imani."

"Mama, I thought we had taken care of everything." He said.

"That's why they see never send a man to do a woman's job. I need to discuss things with Imani that you can't know about."

"Okay. I get it. A surprise for me, huh?"

"Goodnight, Mama," Candace said, interrupting the conversation.

"Hold on, young lady. I need you to hang around for a bit, too," said Mama Re. "Too?" Candace said, looking at Gary and me. "What's going on?"

"I just want to talk to you girls for a minute," she said.

"I have some work to catch up on," said Candace.

"Gary, you go in the kitchen and make sure the caterers leave things as they found them, and they take the leftovers."

"Leftovers? Okay, that's my cue. I think they need to go with me. You, ladies, handle your business; I'm out of here." Gary said, kissing me and then his mom. Candace looked trapped. Mama Re looked at her waiting for her to concede.

"Okay, ma," she said. "I have only a few minutes."

You could have poured me from a glass. The anxiety I had earlier returned with a vengeance.

"Come," she said.

I held my composure and followed Mama Re into the living room. We were barely seated before she started talking.

"I've been noticing some things that have me a bit perplexed. You girls get along so well. That is beautiful, particularly since you are about to be sisters. But, ever since you came back from New York, you have a closeness that appears unnatural even for sisters. Are you sleeping with each other?"

"Mom?" Candace said.

"Don't lie to me. You two are very chummy for black women who just met." She said.

"Candace, your mom has a point," I said, unsure why I was speaking, but I continued. "It isn't the norm, but if Justin Timberlake can bring sexy back, Candace and I can bring back sisterly love."

Mama Re shifted her gaze to me. Before she could speak, Candace spoke up, "The truth is, Mama, I'm prepping her for Gary."

I spit out my tea, laughing. Mama Re did not find it funny. She scolded me with her eyes. Candace rushed her with a hug and kiss.

"Awe, ma, I'm just joking. I'm training Imani, getting her ready to fit into that dress. Do you get it? As a personal trainer, I get up close and personal. We have to spend a lot of time together. It's what I do."

Mama Re's face broke into a smile.

"Candace, that mouth will get you in trouble one day."

"Okay, that's it, goodnight."

That quick, she was gone. I couldn't help thinking that Mama Re had no idea. Looking at the time, Candace asked if she could come over in a couple of days. She had some business to catch upon. I said okay. Even though I knew it would drive me bonkers. I didn't want to create another thing for her to use as part of her rationale for leaving me.

For the next two days, I was on pins and needles. I was ready to spring the seduction on her when it finally came. Candace threw a monkey wrench in my plan. She undressed me from the door. We had sex on the couch, on the floor, on the table, and all that before saying hello. We lay exhausted on the bed, looking up at the ceiling. A part of me wanted to forget why I had

asked her over. The sex had clouded my view, but I recovered quickly.

"This is not why I invited you over," I said. "I'm

sorry. You were looking so good." "But we are done, remember?"

"You're right. I'm sorry. I shouldn't have done that."

"You don't love me. Now you regret being with me?"

"No, Imani. I was saying. Please. Listen. Hear me out."

"I'm sorry for the way I talked to you."

"So, is it true? You used me?"

" It's true I initially planned to seduce you as payback, but when we were at the photo shoot…."

"So the things you said to me at the club and later at the hotel were part of your payback?"

"Let me finish. When I kissed you at the photo shoot, I knew I couldn't go through with it."

"But you did," I screamed on the brink of tears. I jumped up to avoid letting her see me so vulnerable. She followed me, pleading.

"No. I didn't. That was not payback. I have fallen in love with you for real. What happened at the club and the hotel was real."

"How could it be? You told me you didn't love me."

"I lied. I do love you," she said.

I couldn't let her see how happy it made me hear those words. What if she was using that to further her treachery?

"Why the lies then? Or is this another one?" I asked.

"I was scared. I didn't know what else to say. It's complicated. You were talking about telling Gary and us being together."

"We love each other, so why not be together?"

"I love you, but I can't be with you." She said.

"What are you talking about?"

"We can't ride off into the sunset, Imani."

"Why? I'll tell Gary; then we can lay low until some time passes, and then...."

Candace cut me off. "No, Imani, baby, you don't understand."

She cradled me in her arms. "Mama knows Imani. She saw through the bullshit the other day."

"What does she know?" I asked.

"I told her I had feelings for you, but you were oblivious to it." I jerked away from her"Why more lies, Candace?"

"To protect you. I did not steal my vindictive streak. Our family, mama, we have a dark side. Mama would try to hurt you in ways you cannot imagine. As long as she thinks you knew nothing and I back off, she will do nothing."

"I don't need protecting. I need you. I'm still calling off the wedding."

"Imani, Gary worships the ground you walk on. Please don't. It would kill him."

"Candace, it will kill me to be without you."

"Listen, I was your first, and that comes with much responsibility. You will forget about me soon enough. I should have never allowed it to happen."

"You did not hold a gun to my head." "Imani, I'm sorry. He's my brother." "And what was I? Just a piece of ass?" "Don't make this ugly."

"It's already ugly. You want me to marry Gary and

do what? Pretend that I don't love you?"

"No, I mean yes." Candace started pacing."What are you saying? I make you happy, but your brother's and mother's happiness is more important than yours. You're right. You're not the one for me. I need a ride-or-die chick. The wedding is off. I would rather be miserable and alone instead of miserable in a marriage without you."

"Imani, please don't. Gary will not survive this."

"Gary is a grown-ass man." I pointed to the door. I refused to look at her any further. "Get out. I'm done with you and your family."

She pleaded with me. I slammed the door behind her and sat sobbing for hours. I was sad about not being with her, but much more was happening. My fling with Candace pulled the curtain on my insecurities and sexuality. I had never been with a woman before her. I could be confused, as she said. I needed to sort things out.

I gathered myself from the floor and came to terms with what had just happened. I knew that once I announced the wedding was off, my cell phone would start blowing up, and the gossip mill would be churning. Outside of my parents, Gary was the only one who needed an explanation. He deserved to hear it from me. The universe conspired, and there was a familiar knock on the door. It was Gary.

"Hey, baby. I was in the neighborhood. Thought maybe you could use some company."

Gary produced a bottle of wine. "Baby, we need to talk," I said, retracing the last time I was under the influence.

"Not the three words I wanted to hear. But you did meet with Mama today. What's going on?"

"It's not about that. Well, it is kinda." I said.

"Damn. I thought this was a booty call." He said jokingly. My nerves were trying to get the best of me. I had to say it before I chickened out.

"I'm having mixed feelings about my sexuality Gary. It has nothing to do with you. I'm not sure what is happening with me, but I don't think it's fair for us to get married without knowing. I love you. I desire you, but I have to figure some things out. The wedding is off."

"Not the three words I wanted to hear," he said.

"Did you hear me, Gary?"

"I heard you, but I do not believe my ears." Again silence was broken by me.

"I'm sorry, Gary. I wish I could go back in time."

"And do what?"

"I don't know. I'm so sorry, Gary. I wish I could go through with it."

"Imani, honey, I hear you," he said. "I'm floored, but I would never force you to do something you were not ready to do. I appreciate you coming clean now, even though this is late in the game."

"I love you, Gary; I just need some time."

"Take all the time you need. I'll wait," he said. "I didn't mean to hurt you. I'm, I'm..."

I had no words I could say that would make any sense at the moment. Gary helped me out.

"I know you do. Do what you need to do. If you come to your senses and realize I'm the man for you, I'll be right here."

"I'm so confused," I said, grabbing my head. The

pounding of my heartbeat was radiating in my head. It was getting louder.

"Here, take these," he said, handing me an envelope.

"What is it?"

"Our honeymoon tickets."

"What? Stop playing Gary." I tried to give them back.

"Look, woman, don't make me change my mind. I love you. Who knows what the future holds? Take them. Go away for a while when you come back. Let's talk again. Until then, we will put the wedding on ice."

"I need to call everyone. Your mom is going to be so upset, the guest. Oh my God." Gary covered my mouth.

"I'll take care of that stuff. Come. Let me wear the pants for once." He opened his arms for me to enter. I smiled at his gentleness and all I knew about how he loved me. I nestled my head on his shoulder, and I began to cry. So did he.

Gary is a wonderful man. He is the man I wanted

to spend an eternity loving and sexing with. It may sound crazy, but I would have married him if Candace had come with the deal. Together they were the perfect match. However, Candace was off the table. My feelings for them both had me spinning.

Candace was right. I was confused. What was I? Who was I? I needed to sort out my feelings—particularly those that now craved a woman's touch, smell, and closeness. I cried myself to sleep. When I woke up, Gary was gone. The tickets were on the nightstand, with a note.

I love you I called my parents. They took the news as I suspected with many questions. I gave them the cliff notes version and kept it moving.

I checked in on Josiah, bought Gary's ticket, and upgraded to a VIP Jamaica package. I was eager to get away. Within a few short days, I was in a utopia. While there, I met some women who belonged to a secret society or something for women only. They invited me to hang out with them. I was not ready to spend time with anybody in the beginning. I waited until I had enough time before taking them up on an invitation to a bonfire. My last night there was the icing on the cake of my entire trip. One beautiful woman kept watching me from a distance. After about an hour of socializing, she approached me and handed me a card with a number. "Call this number if you don't want this night to end. Don't call as soon as you return home. Wait a few days, then decide."

As quickly as she came, she was gone. I returned home ready for all of the fallout. I had messages on top of messages from the gossip mill. Several came from Candace. One read, "I'm your ride or die. Right here, right now, I'm dying inside. I messed up. Please call me."

"Here we go."

About That Life

KEYSA.

"Six months before graduation and you decide to lose your damn mind."

"It's not that serious Ma"

"Tell it to the judge," she said slamming the summons on the kitchen counter. I pretended not to notice as I eased my backpack off the chair. I wanted to get out of arm's reach before I said another word to Ernestina Jefferson, my mom.

Like hell, it isn't," she continued. You have no idea how hard it can be trying to get a job with a record."

"Ma," My friend Tameka said all they were going to do is talk to me, make me promise not to do it again, and give me community service.

"I don't care what Tameka said. She's not the one who has to take time off to take you to court. And the fact that you are giving me the opinion of someone who's wearing an ankle monitor is not helping my mood right now."

Tameka's my bestie. She caught a charge because she was at the wrong place, at the wrong time. The newspaper said she and 4 of her friends were caught transporting guns across state lines. Tameka was just going for a ride with her boyfriend. She had no clue he was a mule. It was the testimony of the others that helped her get a reduced sentence.

She has to be on house arrest for 6 months, probation for a year, and community service. I didn't do anything like that. I got into a fight and broke the girl's nose so her mom pressed charges. I was defending myself so I'm not worried. However, my mom has lost too many people to the judicial system. I know she's scared for me but I'm not scared of anything. Schools are a joke. I see people on the corner with degrees, begging for money. My mom said they just fell on hard times but if the right opportunity presented itself they could bounce back.

"You keep it up Keysa and you'll be out there with them."

She doesn't understand. I know she pulled herself up but everybody's not built like that. I just want to get through the day and she is tripping.

"Ma, stop sweating me," I mumbled. "Say one more thing. Keysa"

That was the end of that conversation. "Say one more thing" meant shut up while you still have all your teeth. I know where to draw the line. My mom is a problem-solver for powerful people. She is no joke and she knows she raised me to stand up for myself. I have mad respect for her but, I don't care about making good grades or graduating. The system loves educated fools. They throw around scholarships for us to fight for and grants to beg for making you think it's about you but it's really about them. We are pawns on their chessboard. I mean, my grades are good enough for me to get into any college. Maybe not good enough for a full ride but she can pay my way in. Other parents have done it. And let's not forget student loans.

I wasn't always so cynical. I'm just tired of the bullshit hype that says, " Get good grades, get a good job, and work until you retire." In reality, you get an education, land a job, and work until you die. Retirement is a joke unless you have saved thousands of dollars every year since you were born or you get an inheritance. I see retirement-age people working every day in Target and Walmart. A job in fast food or a grocery store is now the endgame. It used to be a stepping stone to landing a better job. Now it's the stepping stone into the grave. College, if I go, would only be to buy a little more time to figure out what I want to do with my life. If I don't go, I still have to figure that out. Either way, it's all bullshit. And, Ma keeps sweating me over a fight. Right now, I'm trying to figure out what to wear to the prom, avoid getting shot, and how get my girlfriend on board with what I want.

Shakira is her name. Our initial connection came on some curiosity-ish she played off as homophobia. I've been queer long enough to know the difference. Shaq was over the top. I was amused as much as I was irritated by her trying so hard to hate me. That was nothing new to me. My mom's job moved us around a lot. Every new school brought new bullies. Shaq was by far the easiest to break. When she found out I had a link with a girl at school, she saw me in the hall and started shoving me. I knew I had to fight. I kicked her ass. Two days of suspension and we became best friends. Like clockwork. Girl meets girl. The girl proves herself. The girl gets the girl.

Shaq's crush on me came with a lot of drama. She wouldn't admit it so she just dissed every girl I talked to. I played it off. She was captain of the flag team, SCA president and she was in the marching band. Her

reputation as an undercover lesbian was not a secret, but no one could prove it. Quite frankly, no one at school cared. Over half the entire place was gay. Shaq identified as straight for appearances.

I on the other hand am a soft butch who is two steps away from being a lipstick lesbian and I like dudes. How is that for unconventional? Shaq freaked when I told her I was bisexual.

"If you are bisexual why do you dress like a dude?" She mocked.

"I like different clothes. I have some dresses at home. I wear them sometimes."

"I never see you talk to guys like that."

"How do you know?" I said. "You are not with me all the time."

"There's no such thing as bisexual."

I was so angry and annoyed at her for saying that and I wanted to punch her but I just shouted, "You are stupid just like everybody else and I don't care what you think." Shaq ignored my obvious agitation and stood up in my face. "You are greedy."

"What do you know and what is it to you?" I said.

Shaq started searching for something to say. Coming up empty she said, "You're a fake." I started laughing.

Shaq laughed too. I knew it was only a matter of time before she would give in to her curiosity. I said I moved around a lot. I've had many curious girls. They ask questions until they finally decide to take a walk on the wild side. It was important for me to have her make the first move. My job was to have fun with it.

"Real talk Shaq, I'm just like you," I said. "I'm not into girls. I have a boyfriend." "That's a cover-up, but you'll come around."

Shaq came toward me as if she wanted to hit me.

"Now you don't want to go there," I warned her. "Remember what happened the last time."

"Whatever man. I ain't like that." She shoved me anyway.

"Okay, this real talk. I wasn't coming on to you. I just meant you have two sides."

"What?" She said.

"Some days you can be so sweet. Other days you are a bitch."

She lunged for me. I took off running. Shaq was not tripping about whether I was bisexual. She was feeling me out. It was time to put her curiosity to the real test.

A few months into our friendship, I started kicking it with a cheerleader from another high school named Kendra. Shaq didn't like Kendra at all. So, I would hardly ever talk about her. Every time I began, Shaq would change the subject. One day while kicking it at the mall, we ran into Kendra and her sister. When she came over to speak, Shaq threw so much shade I got pissed. When they walked away I started talking about how good the sex was with Kendra just to piss her off.

"Did I tell you Kendra is a squirter? I had my whole fist inside of her last night. As I pulled out she ejaculated all over me." I said.

"That's disgusting. You are nasty."

"Kendra was shaking. I tried to hold her down. She raised her hips to meet my lips…"

"Shut up Key."

257

"Why?" I said acting like I had no clue why she was so irritated.

"I don't want to hear about your sex life." She said.

"Since when?" I chuckled.

"You were all ears when I talked about Cassandra."

"I wasn't."

"I bet you liked it?"

"That would be negative. What is there to like about a skank like Kendra?"

"So we get to the truth. It's Kendra. Shaq, I bet if I put my hands in your jeans, right now, your thong would stick to my hand."

"Shut up. I love dick. I'm just trying to understand why you would go down on a female like Kendra." Shaq said.

"I like the dick too. But, this is about you getting off on me talking about fucking Kendra." Shakira started squirming in her seat when I dropped the f-bomb.

"Look at you. Your ass can't keep still."

"I got to pee," Shaq said.

"That's what they all say." I tickled her.

"Feeling a little juicy huh? Go pee."

She smacked my hand away. "You are so nasty." I followed her into the mall bathroom.

"Yep, and you want some of this nasty. All of you curiosity vampires want some. "

Kendra was like that. I gave her a taste, and she wanted more. She's one of those females you know is a ho you can get down with. She's reliable in a pinch. She is not in it for the money. She likes to do it. That's a ho I can mess with.

"Why are you talking like that? You sound like a dude."

"Dude, stud doesn't matter. I'm keeping it one hundred. Ho's like to be talked to like ho's."

"Ho's get paid. You don't even have a job."

"Now you are being stupid. Kendra comes when I call because she knows she will come when I call. " I laughed so hard I almost pee'd my pants.

"Shut up Key," Shaq said holding back her laugh.

"Pimping ain't easy but it sho is fun."

"The bitch is nasty. She is on everybody's dick."

"Wait one minute. Why are you hating on Kendra?"

Shaq was frustrating me but her obvious jealousy would not allow me to ease up. I wanted her to admit she was feeling me.

"What is the real reason you throw some much shade on girls I fuck with?"

"I don't care. Kendra's nasty and everybody knows it." She screamed.

"You're jealous."

"Now who's being stupid?" she said.

"Shaq, you know you can be my top bitch any day of the week."

She laughed, "Kill that noise Key."

"On the real, I know you want me, but it's cool if you want to keep playing."

"That's crazy," she said. "I was only trying to look out for you. Kendra is ratcheted."

"Oh, yeah, right, you are looking out for me. Well, what you don't know is I don't get down with her like that anymore."

"Since when?"

"Stop talking and listen," I said. "She was cool until she tried to play me around all her straight friends. I could rock with that. Until she took it to another level. We were rapping with those homophobic assholes. The subject of lesbians came up. Kendra started dissing lesbians hard. I took one for the team. The next time she called me, I fucked her so hard she couldn't walk right for a week."

"That should have been right up her alley."

"It was, but then I cut her off. She is begging me for it now."

"Damn, I didn't need all of that."

"Say the word, and I swear to God I will drop everyone."

"I know I'm hard to resist, but you will never get any of this." She said trying so hard to be convincing.

She's ready but not yet. I have to crack the whip one more time.

"Pump your breaks Barbie," I said. "You got me

twisted. You are tight, but you ain't my type."

Her face deflated, but she played it off and ran into her house. We had been talking so much that I didn't realize we had reached her house. That was the smokescreen. I watched her go in. She turned and waved at me. Yes, she took the bait. Her ego was too big not to. In my experience, girls who are not into girls don't want to talk about lesbian sex at all. The fence sitters and carpet moochers are open to it wide enough for me to walk in.

A couple of days later Shaq got the itch. She's a noob, a newbie, and wants it all the time now. One little taste of sexual freedom and they go rogue. Typically I would shut it down after the conquest. There was something about Shaq that I wanted. The three T's, are teachable, taste good, and have a long tongue. I was willing to work with that.

Prom night was litty Most of the schools had it on the same night and then they repped at the after party. There were other parties but the one to be at was hosted by the mayor's granddaughter. You needed a special code to gain access. Her parties always attracted a plethora of sexually depraved youth from all walks of life. Let's just say, age was not a factor. There was smoking, drinking, and all types of debauchery-infused activities adolescent minds could conjure. It was bananas. You entered with a date, but by the end of the night, there were only a sea of opportunities.

As soon as I hit the set, I saw Drew aka The Pharmacy. It was not hard to spot him. He was surrounded by Ho's and his boys. He was the type where you knew he existed but you never really saw him unless he wanted to be seen, or he had to come to school for testing. His family was Muslim and they homeschooled. I searched the party until I spotted him. He saw me staring and beckoned for me to come over. I pretended not to understand what he was saying. I like bad boys. Drew was that and more. He lived a dangerous life according to the law. I was intrigued and scared of him at the same time. He stood up and beckoned me again. I saw his six-foot frame draped with dreadlocks that hung past his knees. I started blushing. No one had ever made me blush. I didn't know what to do so I turned away from his direction and started talking to the group that was huddled nearby.

"Hit this," my girl Gina said handing me the blunt. "This is some good shit." She said in between coughs. I took a hit and immediately started coughing.

"It's that damn loud," I said.

"Let me get that." Somebody said.

"What's loud?" Shakira asked.

"Your mouth," I said taking another hit.

Everybody cracked up.

"Here, just hit it." Shakira reached out to take the blunt. Drew intercepted it.

"Damn," Shaq said. She didn't go into her usual rants. She knew the Pharmacy was not the kind of guy you go up against.

"Hold on shawty," he said. "There is plenty to go around."

Drew went into his pocket. He handed a fat blunt to Shakira. "Smoke this while I taste your girl's lips real quick." He put the blunt in his mouth, looked at me, took it out, and licked his lip before taking a puff

"How can you tell if it's my lips you are tasting? "

"Like this." He said pressing his lips against mine.

Drew never hit the blunt. He gave it to Gina and walked away. I stood in shock for a moment. My eyes followed Drew as he disappeared into the crowd.

"Key. What the fuck was that all about? You acting all dreamy and shit." Shaq said. The shade was so thick it got dark in the entire room. Coming back to my senses, I shot her some sarcasm. "You think."

Shakira rolled her eyes and walked off. She knew not to play that jealousy game with me. She and I were a couple, but we agreed to keep it chill until after high school. It didn't take her long to come back. We smoked a little more. The higher I got the more I looked for him. He was gone. Shakira noticed me scoping the room. She snatched me up, and we ducked into one of the bedrooms. There were other people in the room. I could hear their voices. I started undressing Shaq which was always the way sex began with us.

"Not this time," she said."I got this."

"Okay, Betty badass," I said.

Shaq sat me on the bed and slid up behind me. She wrapped her legs around my waist with precision. She slid the straps of my dress down.

"Black lace nice," she said.

"I'm many things. The hook is in the front." I said.

"I know." She unhooked it with her mouth. My breast fell into her waiting hands. The warmth of her mouth felt like an oven as it engulfed my cold hard nipples. Without hesitation she had one finger, then two, then three inside of me. I moaned.

"Um, whose thong is sticking to whose hand now?" Shaq teased.

I moaned. "Mm, you got me." "Who's pussy is this?" she asked. "Yours," I whispered.

"Say my name," she commanded. "Shakira." I moaned.

She slid around me and got on her knees without removing her hand.

"Lay back," she ordered.

I did as I was told. Shaq glided her tongue up and

down my clit as she inserted the remaining fingers inside of me up to her wrist. My moans drowned out the sounds from various places in the room. I closed my eyes. My body was trembling with anticipation when suddenly the door opened. I opened my eyes, but I could only see a silhouette. Instantly I knew it was Drew.

"Come here," I said.

Shakira stopped. She did not notice the door had been opened.

"Who are you talking to?" She said. Drew pretended not to understand my request.

"He knows."

"He?" Shakira tried to pull away to look around. I stopped her. Drew was now standing over us still pretending not to know I was talking to him.

"Oh, you got jokes," I said.

Shakira removed her hand but I would not let her get up. "Stay."

"I don't want to get with him like that." She whispered.

"You don't have to. He's not for you." I stood Shaq up in front of me.

Drew watched as I undressed Shakira and pressed her sweet mango pussy into my face. He stepped back as I slowly lay on my back. Shakira climbed onto my face. I motioned for Drew to come in between my legs. He took over from there, lifting my legs in the air he slowly inserted his penis inside of me. I couldn't see the others in the room but I could sense them watching us. That made it hotter than July in there. Monday morning at school everybody was talking about the party but no one gave details. There were plenty of stares and smiles. I knew Shaq, Drew and I was the subject. I felt like a celebrity. At the end of the day, the mayor's granddaughter caught up to me in the parking lot.

"Did you have fun at my party?" she asked.

"Yeah, it was nice."

"What about Shakira?"

"I think she did. We haven't talked about it much." Oddly enough, Shaq and I had not talked at all since the party.

"Wassup?" I asked.

"I'm having another party this weekend. You should come."

"By myself?"

"Yes, and keep it to yourself."

"You know I'm with Shaq."

"And the Pharmacy from what I could tell." She said.

"That was that night. Not sure where I'm at with that."

"That's why I want you to come over this weekend."

"To talk about Drew?"

"No."

"Okay, what's the deal? You are creeping me out."

"I'm polyamorous," she said.

"Poly who?"

"Polyamorous? That is when you have a multi-person relationship and everybody agrees to only be with each other."

"Why didn't you just say a threesome?"

"It's more than just that. Think of it as a three-person marriage, and you take a vow to be with only each other."

"That's some wild ass shit."

"I'm new to it, but come hang out. I have some friends who can explain it better."

"Sounds like an orgy to me."

"It's not like that. Just a group I belong to that is open to a different way of living."

"Aight, why can't I bring Shaq?"

"Rumor has it she was not too happy with the scene the other night. I don't know if it's true, but the group is private."

"Wow. okay."

"Don't tell anyone. I'll text you the details."

"Details? This is some James Bond shit. I can get with that."

Shakira was not talking to me. Maybe the rumors were true. I knew she had a different view on relationships, and she was very territorial with me. It's unfortunate, but I can't start letting shit get in the way